# SUNDOWN
# HORROR

LARRY NABBS

Read With You Publishing

Text copyright © 2016 Larry Nabbs
All rights reserved.

Published by Read With You Publishing

ISBN-13: 978-1-944710-05-7
ISBN-10: 1-944710-05-1

Printed in the United States of America

# Contents

# PART 1

### Darkness.

The forest was shrouded in mist. A bright full moon hung in the sky far above.

Silence.

Nothing moved. Not a living thing made one small sound. It was as if all life had died and there was only this, the forest, shrouded in mist in the darkness of night.

Suddenly, someone gasped. Timothy sat upright inside the tent. He was sweating. Jenny moaned, moving in her sleeping bag beside him.

"What is it?" she asked sleepily, half opening her eyes to look up at him.

"I . . . I don't know," Timothy replied. "I . . . I was asleep and then suddenly . . . something woke me up."

"Must've been a dream," Jenny said, turning over in her sleeping bag to go back to sleep.

Timothy glanced down at her, then looked towards the tent's opening. Slowly, he moved forward and pulled the tent flaps aside.

He peered out into the darkness. From the silver light of the full moon above he could see across the open clearing where both he and Jenny had decided to put up their tent.

With the mist rolling slowly across the clearing and through the surrounding trees which stood in darkness, the scene before him looked eerie, almost scary.

He wished Jenny hadn't talked him into going on the camping trip. He had heard stories about the forest, stories about things that happened mostly at night, scary stories, but Jenny had merely laughed and accused him of being a child who was afraid of monsters in the dark.

Timothy's pride had been hurt, so he had gone with her to prove her wrong. But now, gazing out at the silent and dark mist-filled landscape in front of him, he wished they had gone to a hotel as he had previously suggested.

Suddenly, something caught his eye. A movement in the darkness between the trees.

He stared towards it, concentrating all his effort on trying to see the movement again, but the darkness covered everything.

# PART 2

Turning, Timothy went back into the tent and groped around in the darkness looking for the torch, careful not to wake up Jenny as she did so. He found it, then went back outside the tent, stood up, and turned on the torch. He shone the beam towards the trees where he was sure that he had seen a movement. The night was quiet and eerie-still as he shone the light from the torch at the trees moving the beam from left to right. At first, he saw nothing, then suddenly his eyes caught another movement. He shone the torch's beam at the bushes beside a tall tree and waited. Suddenly, he heard a growl. It was a spine-chilling sound, the like of which he had never heard before. The bushes moved and dark shapes appeared coming out from behind them, and also from behind the surrounding trees. All at once, dark shapes of human form could be seen moving slowing towards him. They growled with an almost inhuman-like sound that sent a shiver down Timothy's spine. From the light of the torch, Timothy saw the shapes of their bodies and their leg movements, which seemed slow as they walked in jerky-like steps.

"What the hell...!" Timothy said to himself. He raised the torch to look at their faces and a sight of horror made him cry out.

"Aaaargh!" Timothy screamed in shock as he stared at the disfigured faces of the figures moving slowly across the clearing towards him. Their faces were bleach-white with cuts and peeling pieces of skin hanging down from them. One of them, the one who was walking jerkily in front of the others, had green eyes that seemed to shine brightly. This one growled loudly, showing sharp pointed yellow teeth. It had a menacing look on its face as it moved closer across the clearing towards Timothy, leading the others who followed behind him. Suddenly, Timothy saw an arm fall off one of the dark shapes. Timothy screamed again and backed into the tent, falling as he stumbled back against it. Quickly, he scrambled inside and frantically began shaking Jenny to wake her up.

"Jenny! Jenny!" he shouted at the top of his voice, "Jenny!"

# PART 3

"What is it?" Jenny moaned sleepily. "Time to get up already?"

Timothy kept shaking her.

"Jenny! Jenny! Wake up!"

Suddenly Jenny sat upright and pushed Timothy's hands away from her.

"What the hell are you doing?" Jenny shouted. "I mean, like, where's the fire? Have you gone crazy or something?"

"Jenny!" Timothy grabbed her shoulders.

"We've got to go! Right now!"

"What . . .?"

Timothy grabbed her hand and pulled her towards the tent's opening.

"Hey Tim!" Jenny shouted. "Like, what the hell . . .!"

Timothy pulled her out of the tent, and then she saw them.

"Who . . .who are they?" she asked, standing up and pointing at the approaching dark human-like forms moving towards them.

"Jenny! Come on!" Timothy shouted, trying to pull her to the right and away from the tent. Suddenly, beneath the light of the moon, she saw the face of the human-like figure who seemed to be leading the others across the clearing towards them. His eyes shone bright green and his pale white face was filled with cuts and hanging skin.

Jenny screamed.

"Aaaargh!"

She turned quickly, allowing Timothy to pull her forward as they began running across the right of the clearing away from the approaching monsters.

"What the hell Timothy!" Jenny screamed as she ran as fast as she could, grasping Timothy's hand tightly in hers.

"What are they?" she shouted as they reached the end of the clearing and began to run through the trees.

"I don't know!" Timothy shouted back. "Just keep running!"

They ran through the forest as fast as they could, hearing the inhuman-like growls of the monsters behind them.

"They're following us!" Jenny shouted, glancing back over her shoulder.

"Oh my God! What are they?"

"Don't look back!" Timothy shouted. "Just keep running!"

Suddenly, Jenny stumbled over something and screamed. Timothy looked back feeling her hand leave his, then to his horror he saw her falling, slipping and sliding down the side of a slope. Jenny screamed as she fell down the slope towards the darkness at the bottom.

"Jenny!" Timothy shouted, running to the side of the slope and looking down towards the darkness below.

"Jenny! Jenny!" Timothy called frantically.

He heard Jenny's screams coming from somewhere below him. He moved over onto the slope and carefully began making his way down as the growls from the monsters now above him grew louder. "Jenny! Jenny!" Timothy called as he made his way down the slope as fast as he could.

Jenny's screams come up to him.

"Tim! Tim!"

She was now crying.

Finally Tim reached the bottom of the slope and found her.

In the semi-darkness, he could see that she was covered up to her waist in what seemed like thick mud.

"Jenny! Jenny!" Timothy called out. "Grab my hand! Grab my hand!"

He reached out his hand towards her but wasn't able to reach her.

Jenny was screaming and crying as she reached out her hand towards his.

"I can't! I can't!" she cried.

"Jenny! Jenny!" Timothy cried out.

"Can you move?"

"I can't! I can't!" Jenny screamed, now sobbing as her body heaved with emotion. "I'm stuck! Timmy! I'm stuck!"

Suddenly, above him, Timothy heard a noise. As he glanced up, he saw shapes coming over onto the slope and making their way down towards him, their inhuman-like growls becoming louder as they came nearer and nearer.

# PART 4

Timothy didn't know what to do.

He watched in horror as the monsters came down the slope towards him, their growling intensifying the closer they got.

Behind him, Jenny was screaming hysterically and frantically trying to free herself from the mud, but she was stuck fast and couldn't move. Timothy made a quick decision as the leader of the monsters, the one with the bright green eyes, came growling down the slope towards him, he turned and ran. Timothy ran as fast as he could, hearing the growls of the monsters and Jenny's screams behind him.

"Tim! Tim!" Jenny screamed, as she watched him run away. She turned to look at the monsters who were growling loudly and now making their way across the thick mud to get to her.

Jenny gave an ear-splitting scream. Her screams filled the night air as the monsters now reached her and began to claw and grope at her body. Timothy, who was running up a slope on the other side, stopped to turn and look behind him. Even in the darkness, beneath the moon's pale light, he could see Jenny screaming.

She was now completely surrounded by the growling monsters.

Timothy watched for a few moments, his eyes open wide in horror as he stared down at the scene below him. All at once, he saw some shapes circling the thick mud and making their way towards him.

Timothy let out a fearful sound, then turned and ran quickly up the slope on which he stood.

He reached the top, and without glancing back behind him, he began running through the dark forest.

He ran and ran, hearing Jenny's screams disappearing slowly behind him the further he went.

As he ran, he heard growling sounds coming from somewhere in the darkness of the forest behind.

At one point, he was sure that they were closing in on him.

Branches and leaves from trees hit his face as he ran as fast as he could.

Sometime later, Timothy came staggering out of the forest and fell down to his knees on the grass, completely exhausted. He remained still for a moment, breathing heavily, listening and hearing nothing, and then, a few moment's later, he heard the growling of the monsters coming closer again. Once more, fear placed an icy blade into his heart.

Now, shaking with fear, he raised his head to get up onto his feet. And then, he saw it.

# PART 5

The castle loomed up high in front him, dark and ominous in the moon's silver light.

Still breathing heavily, Timothy got up onto his feet. He stared up at the castle in awe. He had never seen anything like it before.

It had spires and towers as if it belonged in some old fairy story, and yet there was something dark and foreboding about it, something sinister that sent a cold shiver down his spine.

He suddenly turned, looking back towards the darkness of the forest. The growling sounds from the monsters, or whatever they were, were getting louder. They were coming nearer. He took one step backwards away from the line of trees as he tried to peer through the darkness, then he took another step backwards, and then he saw them. Timothy let out a cry of fright and turned and ran for the castle as fast as he could with the growls coming closer behind him. Within a few moments he'd reached the large heavy wooden doors of the castle and began pounding at them in a state of fright, not daring to look back.

"Let me in! Let me in! Please! Please!" he shouted, as he pounded at the heavy doors with his fists.

Only a few moments passed, and then the one of the doors slowly creaked open.

The man who looked out was short and hunchbacked.

"Yes?" he said, in a low voice which sounded strangely menacing.

"Let me in! Please! Please!" Timothy cried, now pushing on the door towards the short hunchback.

The man stepped back and opened the door wider.

"The master is expecting you," he said.

Once through the door, Timothy quickly turned and pushed the door shut behind him.

The short hunchback stood watching Timothy calmly, as Timothy leaned against the door breathing heavily.

After a few moments the hunchback spoke.

"This way", he said, turning.

# PART 6

At first, Timothy remained still, leaning against the door and watching the hunchback walk away, then he leaned away from the door and began to follow after him. The hunchback led him across a small cobble-stoned courtyard to the castle's main building. The hunchback opened a door and ushered Timothy inside. Hesitating, but only for a moment, Timothy went inside. He found himself in a large hall. There was a wide wooden staircase leading up in the centre. On the walls, on either side of the hall, there were paintings of men and women. The paintings looked centuries old. The hunchback was walking over to a room on the left of the hall. He opened the door and waited, gesturing for Timothy to enter the room. Timothy looked at him suspiciously, then went inside and saw that he was in some kind of study. Books filled the bookcases on both sides of the room, old books, some of them thick with dust. There were comfortable armchairs, a long table with other chairs around it, and a huge fireplace. A fire roared, burning brightly inside the fireplace as flames leaped as high as if they were alive. Standing just in front of the fire, with his back to Timothy, was a man. He was wearing strange clothes. His clothes were completely black and looked as old as the clothes Timothy had seen in the paintings in the hall.

Timothy stared at the man's back as the man remained standing still in front of the fire. The door clicked shut behind Timothy and he spun round to see that the hunchback had gone.

"I have been waiting for you," the man with his back to Timothy said.

Timothy turned again to look at him.

"Who ... Who are you? What is this place?" Timothy asked, his voice trembling as he spoke.

The man turned to face him.

Timothy gasped as he stared at the man's face. For a moment, he could have sworn that he had seen a red glow in the man's eyes.

"I am Erik Stolz," the man said.

And then he grinned.

Timothy's eyes widened in fear as he saw the two pointed fangs on either side of the man's mouth.

Erik Stolz was a vampire.

# PART 7

Timothy stared at Erik Stolz, "Please sit down," Erik Stolz said, pointing to a comfortable looking armchair nearby the fire. Timothy started to back away nervously. Suddenly, he turned and ran for the door. Erik Stolz watched as Timothy tried unsuccessfully to open the door. The door was locked. He pulled and pulled on it, turning the handle again and again, but the door would not open. After a few moments of trying to open it, he stopped and looked back at the vampire. Erik Stolz had remained where he was standing, watching Timothy with interest.

"The door is locked," Erik Stolz said. "But don't worry, you're not a prisoner."

"If ... If I'm not a prisoner, why ... Why do you lock the door?" Timothy asked, his voice trembling as he spoke.

Erik Stolz moved across to one of the armchairs and sat down. He gestured for Timothy to sit down in the armchair opposite him. Hesitating, and not wanting to get any nearer the vampire than was necessary, Timothy came back over near the fire and sat down in the armchair opposite the vampire.

"What is your name?" Erik Stolz asked.

"T ... Timothy," Timothy said.

Erik Stolz leaned forward, "Timothy," he repeated, as if rolling the name around in his mind. "I'm not going to hurt you Timothy. I know you must be afraid."

"You ... You're a vampire!" Timothy said, staring at Erik Stolz with obvious fear in his eyes.

Erik Stolz nodded, "Yes, I am. I was expecting you Timothy. I told my servant Candor to go and open the door for you. You must forgive Candor, he is a creature of a few words, but he means well. I know what happened to your girlfriend, what is her name?"

Timothy hesitated before answering.

"J ... J... Jenny," he stuttered.

"Ah, a sweet name," Erik Stolz said. "It is short for Jennifer I believe."

Timothy nodded, "Y ... Yes," he said, his whole body visibly shaking as he spoke. "How ... How could you know?" he managed to ask. "About what ... What happened to us, that ... that I was coming?"

Erik Stolz smiled, "I know everything that happens in the forest that surrounds the castle. The zombies have taken your friend Jenny I believe."

"Z ... Zombies?" Timothy repeated, his eyes widening.

"Yes, the zombies. A vulgar bunch. Quite unlike us, of course."

Suddenly, the door opened.

Timothy jerked round to see a young man with blond hair enter, followed by two other young men and two girls. The two other young men had dark hair, as did the youngest of the two girls. The other girl, who looked to be in her early twenties and was strikingly beautiful, had pure white hair. Each of them was dressed in clothes which seemed to have come from the 1800s.

The young man with blond hair walked over to them and stood beside Erik Stolz's armchair staring at Timothy.

"This is my son, Klaus," Erik Stolz said.

Klaus Stolz looked even younger than Timothy. He was possibly in his mid-teens, in contrast to his father, who was maybe in his late forties. Klaus nodded at Timothy without saying a word.

"When do we kill him?" the tallest of the two dark-haired men said, who was still standing by the open door.

Icy fingers stabbed at Timothy's heart filling him with an even greater fear than he already had. He turned to look at the young vampire who had asked Erik Stolz the question. The two dark-haired men and the two girls stared at him, their eyes turning a bright red as they growled showing their fangs. They were obviously eager to taste Timothy's blood.

# PART 8

Erik shot them a glance, "You may leave us!" he said sharply.

One of the girls, the one with pure white hair, eyed Timothy with interest as she walked over to stand beside Erik Stolz. She leaned forward and kissed him, then looked once again at Timothy.

"Can't you give him to us?" she asked in a soft, sultry voice. "Just Annoncietta and me."

She stroked her hand gently across Erik Stolz's face.

"It's been a long time since we had someone ... 'fresh' to play with."

The other girl, with dark hair, younger, and obviously called Annoncietta, moved forward with a grin, "Yes! We have new games we would like to try out! Let us take him down to the dungeon and ... "

"Enough!" Erik Stolz shouted. "I told you to leave!"

The two young male vampires and Annoncietta looked at Erik Stolz with fear in their eyes. They quickly turned and left.

Only the other female vampire remained, still standing beside Erik Stolz and continuing to stroke his face.

"Even me, my love?" she asked, leaning closer to him.

Erik Stolz smiled at her, "Even you, my dear Sinella," he said, lovingly stroking her hand.

Sinella gazed down at him with a pout, then glanced across at Timothy.

"I'm sure you'll love our games," she said softly, with a teasing grin. She went over to him, touched his face gently gazing into his eyes, then said, "Later," and walked out of the room closing the door behind her.

"Forgive my friends," Erik said, now addressing Timothy. "They can be a little ... Er ... impolite."

Timothy stared from Erik to his son Klaus, and then back to Erik.

"I ... I've come to the wrong place!" he said, standing up from his chair.

He turned to leave.

"On the contrary," Erik called after Timothy, as he was about to try to open the door. "You have come to the right place!"

Erik glanced at his son, Klaus, "Please show Timothy to his room, will you Klaus?"

Klaus nodded and walked across the room to Timothy who turned and tried to open the door, but the door seemed once again to be locked.

Klaus reached him, then gently pushed him aside. He reached forward and opened the door without any problem.

"Klaus will show you to your room," Erik said, remaining seated in his chair beside the fire.

Timothy turned to him, "But ... I ... I can't stay here! My girlfriend is ... !"

"Beyond your help," Erik said, staring into Timothy's eyes fixedly. "We'll talk about what you can do tomorrow. As for now ..."

A wolf suddenly howled into the night outside.

Timothy's eyes darted fearfully towards the window and the darkness of the night beyond it.

"Believe me," Erik said, "you'll be safer if you stay the night here."

Timothy looked at him, then swallowed hard.

Erik smiled, showing his fangs.

"Good night Timothy," he said.

Timothy glanced at Klaus beside him. The fear in Timothy's eyes was plain to see. Then he turned and left the room, following behind Klaus.

Two of the vampires who had been in the room, the tallest of the dark haired men and one of the girls, the youngest, Annoncietta, were standing on the staircase as Klaus led him up it. They stared at Timothy fiercely, their eyes seeming to glow red. The young man growled like an animal and showed his fangs as they passed.

Timothy moved past them quickly and continued on up the staircase behind Klaus. When they reached the top, Klaus led him along a corridor to the left and to a room at the far end. All of the time, Klaus had not said a word. Timothy began to wonder if he was mute or impaired of speech in some way.

Klaus opened the door to the room and gestured for Timothy to enter. Timothy moved past him carefully and stepped into the room. He was just about to look around when he heard the door close behind him. Timothy spun quickly back towards the door and tried the door handle, but the door was locked. He turned back to look at the room. It was a large bedroom furnished with dark and very old styled furniture and a huge bed. The bed was already made, its sheets, pure white, seemed to glow in the silvery light of the full moon shining through the open window. Thin white-laced curtains bellowed into the room either side of the window. Timothy looked at the wall searching for an electric light switch, but there wasn't one. The room was lit with an old-fashioned oil lamp and a few candles which stood on the small bedside table beside the bed. Timothy walked over to the window and looked out. Down below, near the edge of the forest, he saw them, zombies, or at least, that's what Erik Stolz had called them. There were possibly ten or twelve of them, he couldn't be sure of the exact number in the darkness. They stood there, completely still, apparently waiting. Waiting for him to go out ... no, ... to 'run' out to them? To run out of the castle away from the vampires and into their hands?

Timothy felt trapped. Outside there were zombies, waiting, and inside, ... inside there were vampires. Were they ... also waiting? Or biding their time for him to get comfortable, before ... he squeezed his eyes shut trying to block the thoughts from entering his mind. After a moment, he opened his eyes and gazed down at the zombies standing in a long line in front of the castle. Occasionally they growled, staring towards the castle's large doors. They seemed to be standing behind a line, an invisible line that they could not cross. Timothy turned away from the window and walked over to the bed. He sat down on its side. Suddenly images flashed through his mind, images of the zombies following both him and Jenny through the forest and growling like crazed animals, images of Jenny falling down the slope into the thick mud at the bottom, images of the zombies going down the slope towards them, and then, as they approached Jenny, who was stuck in the mud, he heard her screams. Timothy's body jerked, and then suddenly his eyes shot open! Had he been dreaming? He glanced down and saw that he was already in bed, lying under the bedclothes, yet he didn't remember getting into bed. He felt that it was only a few seconds ago that he had sat down on its side. He turned and saw a small antique-like clock on the bedside table. It ticked slowly in the silence of the room. Its hands said that it was 2am. Timothy blinked as he looked at the hands of the clock. He was sure that it had only been midnight when he had entered the bedroom. Time seemed to have flashed by without his even realizing it. Suddenly, he heard a noise at the window. The window was still open with its white-laced curtains billowing inwards into the room. He saw a hand appear on the window sill, and then another. Timothy gulped and then sat upright in the bed staring fearfully at both hands.

Someone, or something, was about to enter his room.

# PART 9

Timothy watched, terror-stricken, unable to move, as a dark shape pulled itself over the window sill and into his room. The dark shape landed on the floor softly, its head moving both right and left as it looked around. Timothy froze with fear, gazing around in the semi-darkness of the room for something, anything, with which to hit the intruder and defend himself. He saw the candle in the metal candle-stick holder on the bedside table. He quickly reached out, took out the candle and grabbed the metal holder. He raised it high above his head ready to strike the intruder with it, whoever, or whatever, the dark shape was. The head of the dark shape had now turned towards him. Even though Timothy could not see its eyes, he could feel its eyes upon him, staring at him. The dark shape now began to move across the floor towards him. It had almost reached him when it stopped. It remained still for a moment, watching him. It was wearing a long black cloak. Suddenly, it moved aside its cloak and Timothy saw the crossbow the dark shape was holding in its right hand. Slowly, it raised the crossbow towards him, aiming the crossbow's bolt directly at him. Timothy gasped and inched back in the bed until he felt the wall behind his back, then he stopped moving. He remained frozen, staring fear-fully at the bolt aimed towards him, still clutching the metal candlestick holder tightly high above his head. He stared in fear as the dark shape continued to move slowly towards him, aiming the crossbow's bolt directly at his chest. Thoughts raced through Timothy's mind. Was it a monster? A ghost? But ... with a crossbow? He stared with fear-filled eyes at the dark shape, wondering what, or who, it was, moving slowly towards him. The dark shape stopped moving just a few inches from the bed and stood still. Only Timothy's rapid breathing could be heard in the silence of the room.

"Who are you?"

The voice made Timothy jerk. He pushed himself back harder against the wall behind him, grasping the candlestick-holder tightly in his hand, ready to strike, although, he knew he didn't have much chance against the bolt of the crossbow, but his fear made his thinking unclear, irrational.

"T ... T... Timothy!" Timothy said, stuttering in fear as he spoke.

"Open your mouth! Show me your teeth!" the dark shape said.

The voice which came from the dark shape seemed to belong to that of a girl. Timothy was surprised, but continued to stared at the bolt of the crossbow aimed at his chest. Slowly, he opened his mouth.

"Pull back your lips so I can see!" the girl's voice said.

Timothy did as he was told and pulled back his lips with trembling fingers and showed his teeth. The dark shape holding the crossbow on him picked up a nearby candle that was alight and held it closely to Timothy's mouth.

"Okay," the girl's voice said, after a moment.

The dark shape placed the candle on the bedside table then pushed back the hood that was covering its face.

A young girl with blonde shoulder-length hair stared down at him. Timothy, surprised to see a pretty girl instead of some kind of monster standing in front of him, lowered the candlestick holder he had held raised in his hand.

"Who ... who are you?" he managed to say, his fear now turning to surprise.

"The name's Gloria," the girl said, "and I came here to kill you!"

"Wha ... what?" Timothy stuttered, his eyes widening in fear once again.

"You're obviously not a vampire ... yet! Are you one of their helpers?" Gloria asked, continuing to aim the crossbow at Timothy's chest.

"H ...helper? N ... no! No! I ... I've just arrived! My ... my girlfriend was ... was captured by ... by the zombies!  Out there, in the forest!" Timothy pointed towards the window. "I ... I ran! I found this castle! I ... I asked for help, but they ... they told me to stay! They said they couldn't help ... tonight."

"They're vampires," Gloria said.

"I ... I know! I ... I tried to escape but ..."

"But the zombies are waiting outside for you," Gloria said, finishing Timothy's sentence for him.  "Yes, I saw them," she added.  "I wondered why they were there."

She lowered her crossbow.

"You're in danger here Timothy," she said.

"I ... I'm in danger out there!" Timothy said, pointing once again towards the open window.

"The zombies can't come nearer the castle," Gloria said. "It's like there's some kind of invisible barrier that they cannot cross."

Timothy moved closer to her, "Who are you?" he asked. "Will you ... will you help me? I have to save my girlfriend!"

Gloria stared down at him for a moment.

"It may be too late for that," she said, finally. "The best thing you can do is to save yourself."

She turned and walked towards the door.

"Where ... where are you going?" Timothy asked, suddenly afraid of being left alone.

"To do what I came here to do," Gloria said, turning back to him. "To kill vampires!"

Timothy got up from the bed and ran across to her.

"D ... don't leave!" he said. "Please!"

Gloria studied him, then sighed.

"You have a choice," she said. "Either you stay here alone, or you come and help me."

Timothy stared at her.

"Wh ... what can I do?" he asked, finally.

Gloria took out a pointed wooden stake from under her long black cloak and handed it to him.

Timothy gazed down at the stake he now held in his hand.

"You stab them in the heart with it," Gloria said. "Not that they really have hearts. And try not to get bitten," she added.

She turned and tried to open the door.

"It's locked," Timothy said.

Gloria took a step back, kicked at the door with all of her might, then reached forward and opened it.

"Not anymore," she said, as she went out.

Timothy watched her go with a surprised look on his face, then he followed her out.

They walked quietly along the corridor towards the end and reached the landing beside the staircase leading down. They stopped for a moment, looking down over the banisters at the hall below. The hall was empty.

Suddenly, they heard a terrible, almost inhuman-like scream.

"Aaaaaaahhhh!!!"

"Wh ... what was that?" Timothy asked, grasping the stake tightly in his hands.

Gloria studied the hall below.

"It came from downstairs," she said.

She turned and headed towards the staircase.

"Come on!" she said.

Timothy stood frozen on the spot for a moment, then moved forward and began to follow Gloria down the staircase.

He glanced at the portraits on the wall as he passed them, unable to shake the feeling that the eyes in each of the portraits were watching him.

Gloria reached the bottom of the staircase and stopped. She listened. The staircase creaked in the silence as Timothy came down behind her and stopped at the bottom beside her, listening to the silence.

Suddenly, they heard the terrible scream again.

"Aaaaaaaahhhhhh!!!"

Gloria glanced to the right.

"It's coming from the basement," she said.

Gloria saw the basement door directly under the staircase and ran over to it followed by Timothy. She stopped in front of the door and paused with her hand on the handle, then she turned it and slowly pushed the door open. The door creaked as it opened inwards away from her. Timothy gulped as Gloria moved forward into the darkness beyond the door and started walking down the basement steps leading below. Timothy paused before following her. He glanced around nervously, making sure that no one was in the hall, then he too moved forward, stepping into the darkness, and began following Gloria down the steps towards the basement.

# PART 10

As they neared the bottom, they could see a faint light.

The light was flickering as if it came from burning torches which were caught in a draught. They heard the scream again, this time louder, and stopped on the steps, listening. Timothy was now trembling. His right hand that held the pointed stake was now shaking uncontrollably.

"Do ... do you think this is a good idea?" he whispered to Gloria who had paused on the steps in front of him.

Gloria disregarded his question and raised her crossbow ready to fire. Then, slowly, silently, she continued on down the steps. Timothy watched her descending in front of him. He hesitated, trying to control the shaking of his hands, then he continued, following Gloria down a short distance behind. As they reached the bottom, they heard the scream again. This time the scream seemed to echo around the walls of the basement making it sound even louder and more terrifying. Gloria peered around the wall that ran beside the staircase and she looked across the basement. It was a large basement, dimly lit with candles and burning torches hanging from the surrounding walls. The candles and torches flickered in a draught coming from somewhere on the other side of the basement. Timothy moved quietly forward to stand beside Gloria and also peered around the corner and into the basement. There, in the centre of the dimly-lit basement, he saw three of the vampires he had previously met in Erik Stolz's study. Two of them were the young men, and the third was Annoncietta, the youngest of the vampire girls, whom he had passed on the staircase when Klaus led him up to his bedroom. In front of them, tied to a wooden X-like cross, was a young girl with very short black hair. Her clothes were barely rags which covered parts of her body. She was sobbing and shaking on the cross with her head bowed. The three vampires were standing in front of her grinning, and one of them was holding a knife. Both Gloria and Timothy saw the cuts on the girl's body and the traces of blood which ran down her skin. Beneath her was a bowl partly filled with blood. The lifeless body of a young man lay beside the bowl, his dead eyes staring vacantly upwards, his body, pale, and filled with cuts as if all blood had been drained from him. The tallest of the two male vampires who was holding the knife, moved towards the girl, raised the knife and cut her outstretched arm. The girl screamed again, howling in agony as her body shook and her head moved from side to side. The vampires watched the blood drip down from her arm and into the bowl, and Annoncietta moved forward to lick at the blood from the cut. Both Gloria and Timothy watched the scene in horror. Timothy stood totally frozen to the spot, as if fear had gripped him in its icy grasp. Then, suddenly, Gloria moved forward into the basement. She raised her crossbow towards the vampire with the knife, her eyes blazing with anger.

"You monsters!" she shouted at the top of her voice.

The vampires jerked around in surprise and saw her, their eyes glowing red.

# PART 11

Gloria fired her crossbow.

The vampires, surprised, barely moved.

The silver-tipped bolt struck the tallest male vampire directly in the heart. The vampire howled clutching at its chest. Cracks seemed to appear in its skin as if it was growing rapidly old and then its body seemed to explode in a cloud of dust. The shorter of the male vampires ran forward angrily and before Gloria was able to put another bolt in her crossbow, he was upon her. They fell to the floor, the vampire on top. clawing and scratching with pointed fingernails like claws and trying to bite into Gloria's neck. Gloria screamed, trying to push the vampire off, but the vampire was much stronger. He growled like a wild animal, managed to pin Gloria's arms down, and was about to bite into her neck, when suddenly, it stopped. Gloria stared up past the vampire's face and saw Timothy standing over them. The vampire's skin began to crack, its youthful features began to grow old, and then it exploded in a cloud of dust. Gloria screamed as the vampire exploded over her. She shut her eyes tightly, then opened them and looked up. She was completely covered in the vampire's dust. She saw Timothy standing over her with the pointed wooden stake in his hand. Then there was a scream. It was a loud, inhuman, animal-like cry. Both Timothy and Gloria looked round. They saw the remaining vampire, Annoncietta, the young girl. She was snarling like an animal, her eyes blazing bright red with anger. Suddenly, she rose up off her feet as if she were weightless and flew quickly towards them. Timothy drew his arm back with the wooden stake in his hand and tried to hit her with it as she neared him, but the vampire was too fast and she flew past him, kicking at his face as she went and knocking Timothy down to his knees. Both Timothy and Gloria watched as Annoncietta howled loudly and then disappeared around the corner of the wall, flying up the staircase. Gloria quickly got to her feet. She placed another silver-tipped bolt into her crossbow and then ran over to where the girl was hanging with her head bowed on the cross. Her arms and legs were bleeding from cuts made by the vampire's knife. Timothy stood frozen to the spot, gripping the pointed stake tightly in his hand and staring towards the staircase.

"Help me with her!" Gloria called out as she tried to help the girl down from the cross.

Timothy blinked as if the sound of Gloria's voice had snapped him out of a spell. He turned and ran over to her to help her with the girl. Together, they laid her down on the cold stone floor. Gloria stared down at her and gently stroked her face. She was young, in her teens, possibly eighteen, with a very pretty face. From the black lipstick she'd used on her lips and what was left of her clothes, Timothy guessed that she was probably a Goth, or someone who liked Goth-like fashion.

"Who ... who are you?" the girl asked weakly, as she lay sobbing and staring up at them both.

"Don't worry, we're friends," Gloria said. "Can you walk?"

The girl nodded, "I ... I think so," she said, her body still shaking as she continued to sob.

"Okay," Gloria said, reaching forward to help her up onto her feet.

Timothy bent down and grabbed the girl's arm on the other side.

"What's your name?" Gloria asked.

"J ... Julia," the girl said.

"I'm Gloria, and this is Timothy."

"Th ... there are others!" Julia said. "Down there!"

She pointed towards a dark passage leading off to the right of the basement.

"In cages," Julia added. "Many others ... in cages!"

# PART 12

Gloria led the way across the basement towards the dark passage with Timothy behind helping Julia to walk.

Gloria paused as she reached the entrance to the passage. She took a burning torch which was hanging from the wall and shone it into the darkness. She saw a rough cave-like passage. Spiders and beetles were crawling along the floor and across the walls. She felt a breeze hit her from the other end of the dark passage and glanced at the flames from the torch as they moved in the breeze. She peered into the darkness of the passage, but it was too long for her to see anything at the end.

She stepped forward, gazing down at the spiders and beetles, and went into the passage followed closely behind by both Timothy and Julia. The passage was damp, and there was a terrible odour of death. They walked along it for a few minutes, Timothy glancing both right and left at the spiders and beetles that were crawling along the walls on either side. Finally, they turned a bend in the passage and came to an opening. They stepped down two steps and found that they were now in a large hall. Candles were lit here and there allowing a dim light to shine in the darkness. Timothy gasped as he saw the wooden cages. Some cages were on the floor, and some were hanging from the ceiling. There were at least thirty wooden cages in the dimly-lit hall. Gloria stepped forward slowly, shining the light of her torch onto them. Within each cage, there were human forms badly dressed in rags. They were caged like wild animals. Gloria walked forward shining her torch onto each cage that was on the floor to her left. She saw girls and young men in each of the cages. In one cage, a young man growled at her savagely, grasping tightly at the wooden bars of the cage, trying to get out.

"He ... he has turned," Julia said. "Some of them have turned, others ... are like me. They keep us here for food, they ... they feed on our blood."

Gloria shone her torch onto another cage and saw a girl. Her head was lowered, her hair was covering her face. Gloria stepped closer. The girl suddenly looked up, her eyes were burning red as she growled towards Gloria like a wild animal.

"How long have you been here?" Gloria said, turning to Julia.

Julia shook her head, "I ... I don't know. It ... it seems like months."

Gloria shone her torch onto the next cage and saw another young girl, only this one was clutching her arms around herself and sobbing.

"Some of them have turned," Gloria said. "Some of them haven't."

She looked back at Timothy, "We have to free the ones who haven't turned. We can't leave them here," she said.

Timothy gazed around at the cages in the large hall, "And what if we free the wrong ones?" he asked.

"I Know which ones to free," Julia said.

Gloria looked at her, then nodded. She took out a knife.

"Tell me which cages," she said, "and I'll free them."

Suddenly, they heard a noise coming from the other end of the dark passage they had left.

"I think we have to be quick!" Timothy said, glancing back towards the passage.

Angry animal-like growling sounds were now coming along the passage towards them.

# PART 13

"Quick!" Gloria called out to Timothy. "Help me move this rock over the passage entrance!"

Timothy saw the huge rock near the wall to the left of the passage. He helped Julia sit down on the ground, then ran over to help Gloria move the rock. Together, they pushed it. It was huge and heavy. Both of them grunted as they pushed it with all their might hearing the animal-like growling sounds coming closer and closer along the passage towards them. Finally, the rock began to move. They continued pushing as hard as they could, then the huge rock rolled and went over to the passage entrance covering it. Behind the rock, they could hear the animal-like growling continuing to grow nearer. Through a narrow gap between the rock and the wall Timothy could see bright red eyes moving through the darkness of the passage towards them. Gloria breathed heavily, bending over to catch her breath.

"That should hold them back," she managed to say.

"But not for long?" Timothy said. "Those things are strong!"

Gloria nodded, "I know, we have to hurry."

She went over to where Julia sat on the ground.

"Tell us which ones," she said. "We have to move fast!"

Julia nodded.

With Gloria's help she got back up onto her feet and began to point at the different cages.

"That one, that one, and that one ... "

Both Gloria and Timothy ran over to the different cages that Julia had pointed to. Gloria threw a spare knife over to Timothy and together they began to cut through the thick bindings that bound the cage doors to the bars. From the passage they heard an animal-like growling and scratching noises as the vampires scratched at the huge rock barring their way into the hall. By the time they had finished, both Gloria and Timothy had freed seven people from the cages, some of them young men, and some of them young girls.

"They like us young," Julia said, now beginning to feel a little better on her feet. "The blood is fresh."

"I noticed," Timothy said, studying the seven young people they had just freed.

Each of them was now cowering and shaking with fear as they crouched on the ground.

"You're free now," Gloria said, looking down at them.

"We'll never escape!" one girl said, staring up at her. "They'll catch us! They'll punish us!"

"No on's going to catch you or punish you," Gloria said.

The girl who had spoken stared towards the huge rock covering the passage entrance, and listened to the angry growling and scratching of the vampires on the other side of it.

"I ... I escaped once!" she said, with fear in her eyes as she spoke. "They ... they caught me! Brought me back! They ... they punished me! Punished ... !"

She lowered her head and began to sob.

"I ... I can't go!" she said, sobbing. "I ... I can't be brought back and be punished again!"

Gloria crouched down in front of her.

"If you stay here, you're dead," she said.

"But ... you don't know! You don't know what ... what they do! If you knew ... you ... you wouldn't leave!"

Gloria stared at her, then stood up.

"Those of you who want to escape, follow us," she said.

Slowly, the other six freed captives stood up. The expression on their faces was one of uncertainty and of fear, except for one young oriental-looking girl who seemed calmer than the others.

Gloria picked up the burning torch she had thrown to the ground and walked towards the other side of the hall feeling the breeze. "There must be a way out of here," she said.

She turned to Timothy, "Do you feel that?" she asked.

Timothy went over beside her and raised his hand. He felt a cool breeze.

"Yes," he said. "It's coming from behind this stone wall."

Gloria moved closer to the wall raising the burning torch in front of her. She placed her other hand on the wall and felt along it. Her fingers touched something. There was a slight crack in the wall. She placed her fingers into the crack and felt something inside. Suddenly, she heard a 'click'. There was a rumbling noise, and then the wall began to move. Slowly, it slid to the side mechanically, and then Gloria found herself standing in front of an opening into another passage.

"Wow!" exclaimed Timothy from behind her, gazing at the new opening in the hall. Gloria now felt the breeze stronger than before.

"It has to lead out!" she said.

She turned to the others, "Let's go!"

Gloria stood to one side allowing the former captives to file past her and into the new passage. Julia was the last former captive to enter, and then, just as Gloria and Timothy were about to enter and follow behind them, the huge rock covering the other passage on the far side of the hall behind them moved and the first of the vampires came running and growling angrily into the hall.

# PART 14

Timothy ran quickly into the second passage as the vampires ran into the hall behind them. Gloria instantly aimed her crossbow up at one of the hanging cages with a growling red-eyed occupant and fired. The bolt hit the rope and the cage came crashing down onto the first of the vampires to run into the hall. She turned and quickly tried to find the switch to close the wall on the passage, found it, and then pressed it and ran through the opening as the wall began to close behind her. She ran along the dimly-lit passage, seeing the light from the burning torch up ahead that Timothy had taken from her. As she ran, Gloria quickly placed another bolt in her crossbow. After a few minutes, the dimly-lit passage grew lighter. The passage was now leading upwards making it difficult to run fast. Gloria knew that it wouldn't be long before the vampires opened the passage behind them and followed them through. Back in the hall which they had left, Erik Stolz calmly walked into the hall past the huge rock. which still partly covered the other passage and glanced at the empty cages. His eyes burned red with rage and he growled.

"After them!" he shouted angrily, pointing towards the wall beyond which the second passage lay. One of the vampires quickly ran to the wall and pressed the hidden switch in the crack.

"Bring them back! Dead or alive!" Erik Stolz shouted, as the wall slowly began to move to the side.

Annoncietta, the female vampire who had escaped from both Gloria and Timothy in the basement, was the first to enter the passage. Sinella, the other female vampire, stood looking down at the girl captive who'd been afraid to leave. The girl was kneeling and sobbing at Sinella's feet.

"I ... I didn't go!" she said. "I didn't want to go! Please! Don't punish me! Please!"

Erik Stolz stepped over to her and stood staring down at her.

"Such a good little slave!" he said, running his hand through her hair.

The girl flinched from his touch, then remained still.

"What shall we do with her?" Sinella asked, staring down at the girl.

Erik Stolz grinned.

"Punish her!" he said.

"But ... but I didn't ... !" the girl started to say, her eyes filled with fear as she gazed up at him.

The girl began screaming and begging for mercy as two vampires grabbed her and forced her back across the hall towards the passage partly obscured by the huge rock. Erik Stolz looked around at the humans turned vampire in the surrounding wooden cages.

"Free them!" he ordered. "Let them join in the search!"

Sinella grinned, "Yes, my love!" she said, and turned to open the cages.

"Get them!" Erik Stolz shouted. "Get them all! Do you understand?"

Each of the humans turned vampire being freed glanced down to avoid the brightly red anger burning in Erik Stolz's eyes.

"And any survivors?" Sinella asked, walking back over to Erik Stolz.

Erik looked at her, then smiled, his anger disappearing.

"You may use them for your games, my dear," he said, as Sinella now leaned against him with a grin and stroked his face. "I'm sure your new games are ... very inventive."

Sinella leaned forward and kissed Erik's cheek, "Very," she said softly. "Really ... very inventive!"

Erik chuckled and lowered his head to kiss her.

# PART 15

The small group reached the end of the passage and stepped outside into the fresh air hearing the crashing of waves onto a beach somewhere below them. Gloria moved forward glancing down and saw that they were on a hillside overlooking the sea. The moon shone brightly in the sky above sending silvery light across the waves of the sea in the darkness of the night.

"Which way?" Timothy asked.

"Left," Julia said. "I came here once, there is a path leading down to the beach. If we go along the coast we'll come to a small village."

"They're coming!" shouted one of the young men they'd helped escape. "They're coming!"

He panicked and ran to the right.

"Hey! Not that way!" Gloria shouted after him, and before she could stop them, four more people also panicked and began to run, following the young man who had run to the right.

"Hey!" Timothy called out. "This way!"

He pointed to the path on the left that Julia was now heading towards.

"Let them go!" Gloria said, looking at him. "We have no time to go after them! Let's go!"

Timothy turned and followed Gloria to the left taking the path that led downwards towards the beach. There were now five of them. Julia led the way down the path, followed by Gloria and then Timothy and finally two of the former captives they had freed from their cages, one, a young oriental girl, and the other, a young man. They had just reached the beach when they heard the vampires from above exiting from the passage and growling.

"This way!" Julia said, leading them along the beach to the left. Timothy glanced at the silvery light of the full moon on the sea as he went, thinking that at any other time, this would be a beautiful scene to stand and observe. The growling vampires from above interrupted his thoughts and he continued along the beach following both Julia and Gloria with the former captives behind him.

# PART 16

The vampires ran in the darkness of the night, growling along the hillside as they went, then they leapt high, as nimble as cats, and fell upon the five former captives who were now running across a field. Waves crashed upon the beach just below the hillside as the vampires tore at the former captives' bodies with clawed fingers and bit deeply into their necks with their fangs. The former captives screamed horribly, their screams filling the night, as, helpless beneath the strength of the vampires, they succumbed to the onslaught.

Down below, further along the beach, the small group of people stopped running and turned to look back up at the hillside they had left, hearing the terrible screams of the former captives. Gloria stood for a moment as if she were frozen, staring up at the darkness of the hill behind them, then she turned to the others standing beside her, "Come on! We have to go!" she said. "They'll be coming for us next!"

She took one last look at the hill, then she started running again along the beach followed by the others. Only Timothy remained still, staring up at the dark hillside and listening to the far away screams.

"Oh, my God!" he breathed softly to himself, then he turned and began to run, following behind the others who were now running further along the beach in front of him.

The village looked bleak in the pale moonlight as they moved slowly through its streets. There were no lights, no street lamps anywhere, and it was as quiet as the grave. They studied each house as they walked past. The houses were in darkness, there were no lights behind each window, it was as if each house stood empty of occupants. Gloria led the others through the dark deserted streets until they came to an Inn. The Inn was the only building which had lights inside. The sign hanging outside the Inn moved gently back and forth, creaking slightly in the wind. The sign showed the image of a lamb being slaughtered with the name of the Inn written beneath it, 'THE SLAUGHTERED LAMB'.

"Nice!" Timothy said softly, gazing up at the sign. "Sounds really friendly."

Gloria glanced at him, then looked at the others, "Let's go in," she said. "Maybe they can help us, or at least, we can phone for a taxi or something."

The others nodded and walked forward towards the Inn.

Gloria walked beside Timothy, "I tried my mobile," she said, "but it doesn't seem to work around here."

"I lost mine in the forest," Timothy said.

He looked around at the street as they walked towards the Inn, "I haven't seen one car," he said. "We'll be lucky if this place 'has' a phone!"

Gloria gazed around at the deserted village, "Strange place," she said.

"This is a hell of a strange night!" Timothy muttered to himself as they reached the door of the Inn.

Julia was the first to enter.

Inside was a small group of customers, some of them sitting at tables and talking, others were sitting at the bar. As Julia and the others entered, everybody stopped talking and looked round to stare at them. The silence was almost palpable as Julia, followed by the others, walked across the room. The customers watched them, staring at them intensely, as the the small group walked over to the bar. The barman stopped cleaning the glass he held in his hand and stared at them with a blank expression. Gloria looked around at the scene. The room was dimly lit with old oil lamps and candles. The only sound was that of the floorboards creaking beneath their feet. Gloria looked at the barman, "We'd like a room," she said.

The barman remained still, staring at her.

Gloria glanced Timothy and at the others, then back at the barman, "Maybe two rooms," she added.

The barman continued to remain still, his face expressionless.

"We have money," Gloria said, taking some money from out of her pocket, thinking that maybe it was the ragged clothes of the former captives was what shocked them. Gloria put the money down on the bar and gazed at the barman.

There was a movement to the right, and Gloria abruptly turned to see a fat woman appear from behind a curtain at the end of the bar. The fat woman walked towards them.,

"Oh, my poor dears!" she said, with a welcoming smile. "You look so ragged! What are you doing out so late on such a night?"

"On ... such a night?" Gloria repeated questioningly, as she stared at her.

"Yes!" The woman said. "Didn't you see? A storm is brewing! It's in the air! Can't you feel it?"

The woman held out her hand towards Gloria. Gloria studied her for a moment, then shook the woman's hand.

"My name's Rose!" the woman said.

Her eyes seemed to shine as she beamed a smile at them all. She glanced down at the money that Gloria had placed on the bar, "We have bedrooms upstairs! There is hot water, I'm sure you'll want to freshen up. We have some old clothes we can give you, clothes that previous guests left behind. I'll prepare some hot soup for you, on the house! And you simply must try our cakes! They're very popular in this region! I make them myself!"

She turned, picked up the money from the bar, then waved for them to follow her.

"Come on! The rooms are upstairs!" she said. "They're very comfort-able! You'll see!"

Gloria glanced at Timothy who gave a shrug and smiled, and then the small group followed the woman called Rose across the room towards an old wooden staircase that led upstairs to the bedrooms. The stares of the customers and the barman followed them as they went. Outside, the wind began to blow, rocking the Inn's sign back and forth more rapidly, making the sign creak louder as it moved. Forked lightning shot across the night sky followed by a loud crash of thunder as it began to rain. Only a dim light from the windows of the Inn shone outside onto the dark and deserted streets of the village as the rain now began to pour down heavily.

Klaus stood still in the darkness of street opposite, staring towards the Inn, his eyes shining red as the rain poured down onto him, soaking him in his clothes.

# PART 17

The young man stared with frightened eyes at the pouring rain beating against the bedroom window. He was sitting on the side of the bed in the small but very clean bedroom. Timothy sat on the bed beside him.

"What's your name?" Timothy asked.

The young man remained silent for a moment, staring across at the window. Moments passed in silence, and then he spoke.

"Andrew," he said.

Timothy leaned closer, studying Andrew's eyes. They were open wide, the fear behind them was obvious to see.

"How long ... how long have you been kept prisoner?" Timothy asked.

Once again, Andrew was quiet for a short moment before answering.

"I ... I don't know," he said, answering vacantly, as if his mind were somewhere else.

There was a knock on the door. Timothy turned towards it and stood up. He went across the room and was about to open the door when he hesitated.

"Who is it?" he called out.

"It's me, Gloria," came Gloria's voice from the other side of the door.

Timothy opened it and glanced out at Gloria who was standing in the corridor. He left the bedroom, closing the door behind him, and stood in the corridor looking at her.

"I tried to use the Inn's phone," Gloria said, "but the line's dead."

"Did anybody tell you how far it is to the nearest village or town?" Timothy asked.

"The woman, Rose, said it's quite a long way," Gloria said. "She said there's no taxi, not even a car here, but they do have a horse-drawn buggy that can take us to the nearest town in the morning."

"A ... a horse-drawn buggy?" Timothy repeated, staring at her in surprise.

"I know," Gloria said. "No cars, no phone reception, it's like we've stepped back into another time. This place is strange."

"Strange?" Timothy repeated. "Strange is a weak word for what we've been through tonight!"

Gloria nodded, "I agree," she said.

Timothy sighed, 'Do you trust these people?" he asked.

"I don't trust anybody at the moment," Gloria said. "And you? How are coping?"

Timothy glanced down, "I ... I keep thinking of Jenny," he said, "my girlfriend. I ... I can't just go! Just leave her!"

Gloria studied him, then reached forward and brushed a tear away that had fallen onto his cheek.

"I'll be honest with you," she said. "I don't know if she can be saved, but ... I'll help you if I can."

Timothy looked up at her.

"Who are you?" he asked. "Why are you here? Why did you come to kill the vampires?"

Gloria glance away, then down. She was silent for a moment before speaking.

"They took my sister," she said softly. "Her name is ... " she hesitated,

" ... was ..." she continued, correcting herself, "... Amy."

A sad expression came onto her face as if she were reliving a terrible memory.

"She'd disappeared. I found out that it was nearby, in the forest when it happened. I found her later, in the castle, only, it wasn't her anymore, it was ... she had become a ... a monster, a vampire. It was as if ... something else was living inside my sister's body. I tried to save her but

... she turned on me. There was nothing ... nothing human left inside her. She ... she died, and then ... then I escaped."

Timothy stared at her.

"You ... killed her?" he asked, with a look of both shock and surprise on his face.

Gloria nodded in silence, keeping her head bowed.

"She ... she'd killed an innocent person, another girl they had caught, and was feasting on her blood. There was blood all over her, on her face, on her hands, on her clothes ... she was covered in it. When she saw me, she ... she attacked me, and I ... I had to defend myself. I killed her. I killed her!"

She paused, with her head lowered sadly. "I ... I keep telling myself that it was an accident ... that I had no choice ... after that, I ... I escaped. I vowed to return, to come back and kill them all! Every single vampire!"

Timothy remained still, staring at her and seeing the tears in her eyes.

"I ... I'm sorry," he said.

Gloria looked at him, "Thank you," she said softly. "Maybe ... maybe we should get some rest. We can talk about what we're going to do in the morning."

Timothy nodded, "Okay," he agreed.

He stood watching as Gloria walked back to her room, then opened the door to his own room and went inside.

# PART 18

Beyond the bedroom window, lightning flashed across the dark sky and thunder crashed and rumbled as the rain poured down even harder than before.

Julia, who couldn't sleep, finished off the last of the cakes that the woman called Rose had brought up for them to eat. She glanced down at the young oriental girl they had freed from her cage and who was lying on the bed asleep, then looked at Gloria who was sitting across from her.

"These cakes are great!" Julia said. "You should try one."

Gloria shook her head, "I'm not hungry," she said.

"Poor girl," Gloria said, looking at the young girl asleep. "She must have been exhausted."

"Her name's Yuki," Julia said. "She's Japanese. I think she's only sixteen years old."

"So young," Gloria said, staring down at the young girl.

"Yeah," Julia said. "I'm eighteen, how about you?"

Gloria smiled, "I'm a lot older," she said, "twenty-three."

Julia shrugged, "That's not so old."

"My sister," Gloria said, "she was eighteen."

Julia gazed at her.

"Was?" She repeated.

Gloria glanced down, then nodded, "Yes," she said. "She's dead now."

A moment's silence passed between them.

"I'm sorry," Julia said.

Gloria glanced once again at the young girl on the bed called Yuki.

"She must have been terrified," she said.

"She's ... a little strange," Julia said, gazing across at the sleeping Yuki. "Everyone was terrified, I guess she was too, but ... she seemed calmer than the rest of us."

Julia stood up from the chair she'd been sitting on, then touched her head.

"I ... I feel ... dizzy," she said.

"You must be exhausted too," Gloria said, observing her. "You'd better lie down and get some sleep."

Julia walked towards the bed.

"Yes ... I ... I ..." and then she fell to the floor.

"Julia!" Gloria called out.

She stood up and ran over to her.

"Julia! Julia!" she cried, leaning over Julia and trying to revive her.

Suddenly, a thought hit her. She remembered Yuki, pleased with the cakes that the woman Rose had brought for them to eat. Yuki had been very hungry and had eaten four of them just before falling onto the bed and passing out. Gloria glanced at the empty plate on the small bedroom table that had contained the cakes.

"The cakes!" she said to herself.

She suddenly got up, ran to the door and opened it. She ran along the corridor as quickly as she could and banged on the door to Timothy's room.

"Timothy!" she called, banging heavily on the door. "Timothy!"

The door opened and Timothy looked out.

"What is it?" he asked. "What's happened?"

Gloria pushed past him and ran into the room.

"The cakes!" she said.  "Did you eat them?"

Timothy looked at her, then glanced at the remaining cakes on the plate on the small bedside table.

"No," he said.  "But ... Andrew had three.  Why?  What is it?  What's wrong?"

Gloria went over to the bed and looked down at Andrew who seemed to be fast asleep.

"The cakes!" Gloria said, turning back to Timothy.  "I think they're drugged!"

Timothy stared at her.

"Drugged?" he repeated.  "But ... "

Suddenly, his eyes opened wider.

"Oh, my God!" he said.  "The people in the bar!  This place ... !"

"They're all in it together!" Gloria said.  "They're working with the vampires.  We have to find the buggy.  We'll carry Andrew, Yuki and Julia down to it and leave here ourselves, now!  We can't wait till morning!"

"But there is no buggy," said a woman's voice behind them.

They turned and saw Rose standing in the open doorway.  She was staring at them with a smile on her face.

# PART 19

Both Gloria and Timothy stared at the woman called Rose as she stood in the doorway with what looked like an old shotgun aimed at them.

"Wha ... what are you doing?" Timothy asked, not taking his eyes off the shotgun.

"She's with them," Gloria said, staring directly into the woman's eyes. "She's with the vampires."

Rose's smile widened, "Very clever," she said. "I take it you to didn't eat the cakes?"

"The other villagers," Gloria said, "are they involved too?"

"Yes," Rose said. "Everyone in the village is involved, we all work for the vampires. They leave us alone, especially if we bring outsiders for them to feed on. Outsiders like you!" she said. "They're always in need of fresh blood. They'll be here soon, I've already sent word, so you may as well sit down and get comfortable while you wait, you're not going anywhere. If you try to rush me, I'll blast you apart! This weapon may look old, but believe me, it still works."

"You're just as bad as they are!" Timothy said, glaring at her hatefully. "You're just as much a monster!"

"But I'm alive!" Rose said.  "And the people in this village are alive! Because of what we do!"

"And ... and you can sleep with that?" Timothy asked, as he stared at her in shock.

Rose shrugged, "Of course.  It's just a matter of survival.  Ours ... or yours."

Suddenly, they heard a noise.  Rose looked to her right.

"What are you doing here?" she asked, speaking to someone in the corridor, who neither Gloria nor Timothy could see.

All at once, there was a loud roar and a movement so fast that it seemed like a blur to their eyes.  Rose screamed, her weapon clattered to the floor, and then they saw Klaus kneeling over Rose's unconscious body. Timothy gasped as Klaus turned to look at both him and Gloria, his eyes glowing bright red.

# PART 20

As klaus stood up to face them, Timothy took a step back.

Gloria remained where she was standing.  Slowly, she took out her knife.  Klaus remained still, staring at them both, then he spoke.

"You're in danger," he said, with a soft-spoken voice.  "You must come with me."

Timothy stared at him, both surprised by the fact that Klaus could speak, and by what he had just said.

"Why would we trust you?" Gloria asked, holding her knife ready in case Klaus was about to attack them.  "Why would  you help us? You're one of them! You're a vampire!"

Klaus stared at them both for a moment, then shook his head, "I'm not like them." he said.  "Believe me, if you value your lives, you must come with me, now! They'll be here soon."

Timothy glanced back at Andrew's unconscious body on the bed, "Our friends!" he said.  "We ... we can't just leave them!"

"The other two are also unconscious, I gather?" Klaus asked, looking at Gloria.

Gloria nodded, "Yes ... they're in the other room."

"Then I will help you," Klaus said. "We'll each carry one of them. Quickly! I have a carriage waiting in a street nearby! We'll leave by the back entrance!"

Gloria stared at him distrustfully, then walked towards him, still holding her knife ready in case it was a trick. Timothy turned and picked up Andrew from the bed, putting him onto his shoulder to carry him. Gloria, still staring at Klaus, slid past him out of the bedroom and into the corridor. She stepped over Rose's unconscious body and went quickly back to her room. Klaus followed closely behind her as Timothy, still carrying Andrew on his shoulder, knelt awkwardly in the corridor and picked up Rose's shotgun.

# PART 21

It was pouring with rain as they exited the back entrance to the Inn, each of them carrying a person who was unconscious. As they made their way along the backstreet, they heard growling sounds coming from somewhere behind them. They turned, and in the darkness saw several dark shapes running towards them.

"Go!" Klaus shouted, dropping Julia from his shoulder to the ground. Timothy turned to run along the rain-soaked street, splashing in puddles as he went, while Gloria hesitated. She decided to stay with Klaus and fight. She lay Yuki on the ground, then took her crossbow. She raised it and fired the first bolt as the growling figures as they came nearer. The bolt tore through a vampire's chest piercing its heart and the vampire seemed to freeze in its tracks, its skin began to crack, and then it exploded in a cloud of dust. Klaus ran towards the other vampires, growling as he threw himself against them knocking two of them over, and then with a special knife, cut the throat of another. Other vampires appeared from the darkness as Klaus fought. Klaus threw one over his shoulder and kicked another while Gloria fed another bolt into her crossbow and fired hitting yet another vampire who disappeared in a cloud of dust. She was about to reload her crossbow when a vampire jumped at her knocking her back and onto the ground. The vampire growled showing its fangs, then leapt towards her. Suddenly there was a loud explosion. The vampire cried out and jerked back before reaching her. Parts of its body began to crack, and then the vampire exploded in a cloud of dust just above her. Gloria looked around and saw Timothy aiming Rose's shotgun at another vampire who was now running towards him. Timothy fired again hitting the vampire who immediately exploded and disappeared.

"Right in the heart!" Timothy said, seeming to be pleased with to himself. "This thing must be loaded with silver!"

Gloria had barely got to her feet when another vampire ran towards her. She avoided his attack, spun round and caught the vampire in the throat with her silver knife. Timothy, with no more shots left in the shotgun, ran forward grasping the shotgun in both hands to use it as a club. Gloria picked up her crossbow and fired a bolt hitting another vampire in the chest. She glanced across to Klaus who was fighting off two vampires at the same time. More vampires ran out of the darkness towards them.

"We have to go!" Gloria called out. "There are too many of them!"

Klaus cut the throat of one of the vampires attacking him. The vampire exploded in a cloud of dust as Klaus turned and kicked the other.

"Come on!" Gloria shouted.

Klaus turned to Julia who was still lying unconscious on the ground and quickly pulled her up onto his shoulder, then ran as fast as he could as Gloria did the same with Yuki. Timothy saw a vampire running towards Gloria. He ran towards it, swung the shotgun at its head and the vampire fell back with a cry onto the ground. Timothy looked up and saw the other approaching vampires. He glanced down at Andrew lying unconscious on the ground and realized that he had no time to save him. He hesitated, then turned and ran as fast as he could along the dark rain-soaked backstreet seeing both Gloria and Klaus running further along the street up ahead. Klaus turned the corner and reached the carriage which had two black horses harnessed in front of it. He lay Julia in he carriage and got into the driver's seat as Gloria and Timothy came running around the corner to join him. Timothy helped Gloria put Yuki into the carriage, then they both quickly jumped inside. Klaus cracked a whip above the horses startling them and forcing them to move forward quickly. Just as the carriage started to pull away, several vampires ran around the corner towards them growling savagely. Gloria quickly loaded a bolt into her crossbow and leaned out of the carriage to fire back at them. The bolt hit the first vampire in the chest who disappeared in a cloud of dust. The carriage now sped deathly-quick along the dark and sinister looking village streets as the rain poured down and lightning streaked across the blackness of the night sky above them.

# PART 22

The carriage rode through the rain-swept night as lightning streaked across the sky and thunder crashed and rumbled overhead.

The had left the village, and Klaus finally pulled the horses to a stop on a muddy track that ran through the forest.

"We're here!" he called back, getting down from the carriage.

"Where are we?" Timothy asked, looking out at the dark surrounding trees.

Klaus reached into the carriage to pick up Julia and place her on his shoulder.

"Follow me!" he said.

Both Gloria ad Timothy glanced at each other as Klaus began to carry the unconscious Julia through the rain and between the trees.

"Do you trust him?" Timothy asked.

Gloria placed another bolt into her crossbow, "It's best to be on our guard," she said.

Timothy nodded, "Right," he said, agreeing with her.

Gloria got out of the carriage holding her crossbow ready to fire and Timothy followed her out.

"I'll take her," Timothy said, leaning back inside the carriage to pick Yuki up and put her onto his shoulder.

He turned and followed Gloria through the trees in the same direction that Klaus had taken. Together, they walked in the pouring rain, following Klaus through the forest, suspiciously prepared for anything that may happen. Klaus led them to a rocky hill in the forest at the base of which was a cave.

He turned to look back at them, "In here!" he said.

They followed as he walked out of the rain and into the darkness of the cave. Both Gloria and Timothy glanced at each other as they entered, neither one of them feeling comfortable with the situation. The cave was dry and surprisingly warm. Further inside, Klaus lit torch that was hanging from a fixture on the cave wall. He held the burning torch up in front of him as he walked. The cave was wide with rocks scattered around on either side of them and at the end they saw a passage. Klaus headed across the cave towards the passage still carrying Julia on his shoulder.

"This way," he said, glancing back at them.

Once again, Gloria and Timothy glanced at each other. Together, they walked across the cave and entered the passage following behind Klaus. The passage was dark, but after a moment, with each step they took, an electric light came on above them, lighting up the passage as they made their way along it. Both Gloria and Timothy looked up at the lights curiously, realizing that this was no ordinary cave or passage. They seemed to have walked along the passage for about five minutes before they came to the end and found themselves in a huge cavern. There were lights everywhere, above on the cavern's ceiling and on the the walls surrounding them. But what surprised Gloria and Timothy most, was the large glowing, orange coloured, triangular object standing in the centre of the huge well-lit cavern floor in front of them. Both Gloria and Timothy stood staring at the strange looking object in amazement.

"What is it?" Gloria asked, coming up beside Klaus, who now lay Julia gently down on the cavern floor.

"That," said Klaus, "is a Time Machine."

# PART 23

Timothy gently lay Yuki down on the cavern floor and walked slowly over to the large glowing triangular object, staring at it in both disbelief and shock.

"You're kidding!" he said, as he reached it.

Klaus moved forward, followed by Gloria.

"Not at all," Klaus said. "It's a Time Machine. At least … that's what it will be, when it works."

Timothy reached out and touched it.

There was a faint vibrant humming sound coming from it.

"What do you mean … when it works?" Gloria asked.

Klaus glanced at her.

"My father … he'd been working on it for a long time, before he … changed."

"Your father?" Gloria said. "You mean, that monster called Erik?"

Klaus stared at her for a moment.

"He wasn't always a monster," he said. "Before, he was a scientist, an explorer. Things happened, bad things. Over the years, he worked on ... designed, this time machine, so he could go back and change what had happened, but ... the illness was too strong for him, and finally, he stopped."

"By illness, you mean, him being a vampire?" Gloria asked.

Klaus nodded.

Timothy turned to look at him, "So, why aren't you like him?" he asked.

"I will tell you," he said, "but first, let us go inside. There are living quarters, it will be more comfortable to rest."

They watched as Klaus turned, went over to Julia, and once again picked her up and placed her onto his shoulder. He then walked back to the strange triangular object, touched something on the smooth glowing orange wall, and then a door slid silently open. Still carrying Julia, he stepped inside. Timothy glanced at Gloria raising his eyebrows, then went back to pick up Yuki. Gloria watched him pick up the young girl, then turned and followed Klaus through the open doorway. Timothy reached the doorway and hesitated, staring at the large glowing triangular object, then he took a deep breath and went inside, the door sliding quietly shut behind him.

# PART 24

Inside the strange object, there was a large brightly-lit circular space with a passage leading off to other areas. The surrounding walls seemed to be filled with light. Running along the wall to the left was a wide and long comfortable looking sofa-like seat fixed in place, and in the centre of the room stood a large circular machine with coloured lights glowing in various glass-like tubes on a circular control panel with levers and coloured buttons, some of which flashed on and off.

Julia now lay unconscious on the wide sofa-like seat where Klaus had placed her.

Timothy gazed around the strange looking control room in awe, then walked over to where Julia lay and placed Yuki gently down beside her. Klaus sat down on the wide sofa observing both Gloria and Timothy as they walked around the large brightly-lit control room staring at everything with expressions of both shock and surprise on their faces, then he took something out from one of his pockets. It was a small container. He opened it, took out some of the white cream inside, and then began placing the cream on the cuts on Julia's arms and legs.

"What are you doing?" Gloria asked, watching him suspiciously.

Klaus looked at her, "It's a medicine, it will help her cuts to heal," he said.

Timothy glanced up at a screen on one wall which showed the view of the cavern outside, "So," he said, "this is a Time Machine?"

"Yes," Klaus said. "But like I said, my father ... changed, before he could complete it."

Gloria looked back at Klaus, then went over and sat down on the wide and long sofa-like seat beside him.

"Why was he building it?" she asked.

Klaus looked into her eyes, then glanced down sadly.

"To help you understand," he said, "I must tell you what happened long ago, before I was born."

Timothy went over to them and sat down staring at Klaus.

"It started on another planet," Klaus said. "Far away, in another universe ... "

He paused, gathering his thoughts, his memories of the story which had been passed down to him.

Both Gloria and Timothy remained quiet in the silence, waiting for him to continue.

"My father and his brother came from another planet," Klaus said. "They were scientists, explorers, exploring other worlds. They went to a planet which they called 'Genera'. Its atmosphere seemed hospitable and they began exploring it. At first, there were no problems, then they discovered that the planet was inhabited by two types of dominant life forms. There were creatures, human-looking creatures, who killed and drank their victims

blood ... "

"Vampires," Gloria said.

"Yes," Klaus agreed, glancing at her.

"And the other dominant form of life?" Timothy asked.

"The others were more beast-like creatures, similar to the zombies you met. Both forms of life were at war with one another. My father and his brother had split up taking two separate patrols to explore two different parts of the planet. My father came into contact with the vampire-like creatures, and his brother, my uncle, met the others. Most of the people in the two patrols were killed, but both my father and his brother managed to escape with a few others and made it back to their spaceship. But they had been bitten, and it was obvious that they were changing. The other members of the crew, who had remained on the spaceship, isolated them in case they became infected by the same strange illness that those who had returned from the two patrols were suffering from. They had a decision to make. Kill them, or leave them stranded on some distant planet. Both my father and his brother, and a few of the others who had been bitten, were notable scientists, even heroes, back on their own planet. The crew, who respected them immensely, finally came to the decision not to kill them and instead, leave them behind on a different planet. The nearest habitable planet was Earth, so they brought them here."

"To infect the people on this planet?" Timothy asked, shocked at the idea.

Klaus shook his head, "Not really. You see, they built a dome around the area surrounding this forest. It's invisible, you can't see it, you can't even touch it or feel it, but it's there. Those who are infected cannot go out, cannot leave and go into the outside world, so the infection, both infections, cannot spread. It's like a prison, we are trapped inside. But ... those who are not infected can enter, just like you did, and you can leave."

"You mean ... if we remain free from infection, we can escape?" Timothy asked. "But ... if we get infected ... we ... we can't leave?"

Klaus nodded "Exactly," he said. "My uncle's infection, the zombie infection, was stronger than my father's. Very fast, he became like a ... a beast. But my father kept his mind, at first, just as it had always been, but he had a craving for blood, human blood, and it seemed that the more people he killed and the more blood he drank, the more he changed. One day, he met a woman and fell in love, and so that they could live together, he turned her into a vampire. That was my mother. After I was born, the infection seemed to weaken her. She made my father promise never to let me drink human blood. Over the years, I have seen my father change. His thirst, and the others thirst for human blood became stronger, they began to lose all feelings, became devoid of compassion. At first, my father wanted to build this time machine to go back and change everything. He had almost completed it, but then, he stopped, and I realized that he was not the same anymore."

"And you've never drunk human blood?" Timothy asked.

Klaus shook his head, "Never," he said.

"But he's still your father," Gloria said. "Why would you help us?"

Klaus looked at her. There was something in his eyes, something strange as he gazed into hers.

"I met someone," he said. "A girl. A normal girl who came from the outside, and ... I fell in love with her. My father said that I should change her, turn her into one of us, turn her into a vampire if I wished to be with her, but ... she was so pure, so gentle, I ... I didn't want her to change. The others ... they ... " Klaus glanced down, a sadness coming onto his face as if the pain of remembering was too much, " ... they changed her. They said they did it for me, they said I was too weak. After she became one of us, she had a thirst for blood. I tried to control her, tried to give her animal blood, but the others gave her human blood, and then she began to crave

for it, wanted to kill for it, just like the others, and then ... then she wasn't the same girl anymore ... not ... not the same girl I loved."

"She became a monster," Timothy said.

Klaus remained silent, gazing down and thinking back to the girl he had loved, then he nodded.

Both Gloria and Timothy stared at him in silence. Gloria reached into her pocket and pulled out a photograph.

"Is this the girl?" she asked, with a tightness in her throat as if she were holding back tears.

Klaus looked at the photo in Gloria's hand. He stared at it, then tears came into his eyes.

"Yes," he said softly.

"Her name was Amy," Gloria said.  "She was my sister."

"I know," Klaus said, looking up at her.  "You have the same eyes," he said.

# PART 25

Gloria placed her hand over her eyes trying to keep back her tears.

"My sister went missing," she said.  "I know she came into this forest, so I came to find her.  What I found was ... was not my sister, but a monster, a vampire!  I ... I tried to help her escape, but ... she turned on me.  We fought, and ... and then she ... she exploded into dust! I ... I didn't mean to ..."

Her body shook as she sobbed.

"Later, when I was running through the forest, I came across a young girl.  She was running, terrified!  She ran into me.  They're coming! she said.  They're coming! I asked her who, and then I saw them, Zombies! Together, we ran.  But the girl stumbled, and before I could go back and help her, they were already upon her! I ran! I ran, and ran, and ran! I couldn't stop running! And then, I was out of the woods and running along a road."

"The Zombies," Klaus said, gazing down.  "The vampires have an agreement with the zombies, my uncle's clan.  We don't go into their territory, and they don't go into ours.  Neither clan wants a war.  When you were escaping, you went into their territory, so no vampires could follow you."

"When I escaped," Gloria said, "I told everyone I could about what had happened, I told people about the vampires and the zombies, but nobody believed me, they all thought that I was crazy. The police came to investigate, found nothing and then quickly left saying that I must have imagined everything and that my sister had probably run off somewhere.  I discovered that there were other disappearances in the same area. That's when I decided to come back and kill as many of these monsters as I could, starting with the vampires."

"Just you?" Timothy asked, staring at her in surprise.

Gloria looked at him.

"When you're angry ... when you're full of hate ... all rational thought gets lost, I just wanted ... I just wanted revenge!"

"I ... I'm sorry about your sister," Klaus said, gazing into Gloria's eyes. "I ... I loved her."

He glanced down sadly.

"Now you know why I want to help you," he said, softly.

Gloria stared at him, her emotions were in a turmoil, she didn't know if she wanted to kill him for being a vampire, or take her into her arms and console him.

Timothy stood up glancing around at the Time Machine.

"What if ... what if we could get this thing to work?" he said. "What if it were really possible to go back in time? We could ... change everything!"

Klaus stood up, "Only my father has the knowledge to do that," he said.

"What if you talk to him?" Timothy asked. "Try to convince him?"

Klaus shook his head, "I told you, he has changed. He's not the same as he was. He would never listen to me."

"There must be a way!" Timothy said. "There must!"

Julia groaned.

Each of them looked towards her.

Julia's hand went up to her head and her eyes blinked open.

"Wh ... where am I?" she asked, gazing around at the brightly lit walls of the Time Machine, and then up at Gloria.

"Don't worry, we're safe," Gloria said, placing her hand gently on Julia's shoulder.

Timothy went over to the console with the controls and stared down at the various levers and colourful buttons which were flashing on and off.

"What if it works?" he said. "I mean ... has anyone ever tried it?"

He reached out to press a button.

"Don't touch that!" Klaus cried out, moving forward to stop him.

But it was too late, Timothy had already pressed the button. The machine started to vibrate, as a strange mechanical whirring noise sounded, getting louder and louder.

# PART 26

Julia sat up, looking around.

"What is this place?" she asked, gazing around in amazement. "What just happened?"

Timothy was standing over the console staring up at the screen on the wall. The machine's whirring noise had now stopped.

"I think ... I think we just travelled somewhere!" he said.

Klaus moved quickly around the console checking everything.

"My father explained things to me," he said. "He told me that it wasn't ready!"

Timothy looked at him, "Maybe he lied to you," he said. "Maybe this machine works after all!"

Gloria stared up at the screen and stood up moving closer to it. The screen showed a view of a clearing in the forest. It was dark as if it were still night time.

"We're in the forest," she said.

Klaus checked the time clock on the console.

"We're still in the same time period," he said. "We must have just ... moved, from one place to the other."

Julia stood up, still holding her head and feeling slightly dizzy.

"Will someone please tell me what's going on? Where are we? How did we get here?"

Gloria turned to her and spoke quickly, "You were drugged at the Inn," she said. "We had to escape, and now we're here ... in a Time Machine, but apparently it doesn't seem to work!"

Julia blinked as she stared at her.

"A ... a Time Machine?" she repeated, in disbelief.

Suddenly she saw Klaus and gasped. She raised a finger, pointing towards him, her eyes widening as she stared at him.

"He ... he's one of them!" she said. "He's a vampire!"

Timothy turned to her, "Don't worry, he's on our side."

He turned back to look up at the screen.

"I know that place," he said.

He looked at Klaus, "Is there a control to move the screen to the left a little?" he asked.

Klaus nodded and touched a control on the console and the screen moved to the left.

"There!" Timothy cried out, pointing up at the screen. "Do you see that? That's my tent! We're in the same place where the zombies took Jenny, my girlfriend!"

"I know that clearing," Klaus said, looking up at the image on the screen. "It's near the zombies' lair. There is a large hole nearby which leads underground, it's where they live."

Timothy turned to him.

"Open the door!" he said.

"What?" Julia asked, standing up and moving forward towards the console. "You want to go out there? That place is crawling with zombies!"

"My girlfriend's there!" Timothy said.

"Then she is lost to you," Klaus said.

Timothy leaned onto the console staring into his eyes, "I said, open the door!"

Klaus studied him for a moment, then touched a switch on the console. There was a humming sound, and then the ship's door opened, sliding silently to the side.

"I'm going with you!" Gloria said, moving forward.

Timothy looked at her, then nodded, "Good!" he said. "I'll probably need some help!"

Klaus sighed, then he also moved forward, "I'm coming too," he said. "You're going to need weapons."

"A stake in the heart won't do it?" Timothy asked, taking the wooden stake that Gloria was handing to him.

Klaus shrugged, "It might slow them down."

"Are there any weapons on this ship?" Gloria asked.

Klaus thought for a moment, then nodded, "Yes! ... Yes, there are!"

He turned and walked over to the brightly lit wall on the other side of the ship, "I'd almost forgotten about these!" he said. He pressed something on the wall and a panel slid open to reveal what looked like a large cupboard with various things inside including clothes and weapons. Klaus found what he was looking for and took out three large swords, the blades of which shone in the light from the ship's surrounding walls.

"Swords?" Gloria said, in a surprised voice as she moved forward to take one.

"My father left them here in case we were attacked by zombies," Klaus said.

He handed a sword to Timothy.

Klaus looked at him, "You have to cut off their heads to kill them." he said.

Timothy nodded, "I'll cut anything, as long as I can get Jenny back!" he said.

"What ... what about me?" Julia asked, looking at them.

Gloria turned to her, "You stay here," she said. "Someone has to stay with Yuki."

Julia glanced round and looked at Yuki who was still lying unconscious on the wide sofa-like seat. She turned back to Gloria and nodded, "Okay," she said.

Klaus went over to her, "Look, these a are the controls to open and close the door and to operate the screen," he said, showing Julia the controls on the console. "Don't open the door for anyone but us!"

Julia looked down at the controls and nodded, "Got it!" she said.

Timothy turned back to the open door. He paused, staring out at the darkness beyond it.

"It'd be a lot easier if we could go back to 'before' the zombies took her," he said.

Klaus shook his head as he moved forward towards the door, "I'm not sure if we can do that," he said. "If the machine can really go back in time, we could end up anywhere."

"He's right," Gloria said. "We'll just have to take what we've got."

Timothy glanced at them both, then nodded.

"Okay," he said. "Let's go kill a few zombies!"

Timothy turned and left the ship, followed by both Gloria and Klaus. Julia watched them go, then closed the door after them.

# PART 27

The storm had passed as Klaus now led the way, moving silently through the rain-soaked forest. Moving between two tall trees, Klaus suddenly stopped.

"It's here," he whispered, glancing back at Gloria and Timothy.

They moved up beside him and looked down to where Klaus was pointing. The dark sky above was now clear, and beneath the silvery light of the full moon, they saw a large hole in the ground at the bottom of a slope.

"I came here once before," Klaus said. "When the truce was made between my people and the zombies. It leads into very deep passages and caverns, but there is one cavern in particular which is much larger than the others, that's probably where they are."

A noise sounded to the left.

Suddenly, two zombies appeared pushing through the bushes towards them and growling.

"Their heads!" Klaus shouted, running towards one of the approaching zombies. "Cut the heads!"

Gloria ran towards the second zombie as Klaus quickly beheaded the zombie on front of him. Klaus glanced round to see Gloria do the same. Timothy stood frozen on the spot grasping the handle of his sword tightly and staring at the zombie heads as they fell to the ground, rolling. Suddenly there was a noise behind him. He jerked round and saw a third zombie moving towards him. Without a moments thought, Timothy stepped forward, swung his sword and cut through the zombie's neck, cutting off its head with one blow of the sword's sharp blade.

Klaus came over to him and patted him on the shoulder, as Timothy remained still, staring down with a look of horror on his face at the head which now lay at his feet.

"Well done," Klaus said.

"What were they?" Gloria asked. "Guards?"

Klaus looked at her, "Probably," he said.

He glanced down at the large hole at the bottom of the slope.

"Well, are you ready?" he asked.

Gloria looked at Timothy.

"Timothy?" she said.

Timothy blinked, then forced his eyes away from the head at his feet.

He glanced at both Gloria and Klaus, who were standing in front of him and looking at him strangely.

"Let's go!" Timothy said suddenly, with a determination in his tone of voice.

He moved past them and began to walk down the slope.

Both Gloria and Klaus exchanged glances, and then they followed him down the slope towards the large hole at the bottom.

# PART 28

The hole was dark and damp with a terrible rotten smell as they walked along the hole's narrow passage which sloped downwards. Here and there, torches were fixed to the walls, their flames flickering in the breeze from the hole's opening behind them.

"It smells terrible!" Gloria complained.

Klaus glanced round at her and smiled, "They're not the cleanest of life forms," he said.

"It smells like rotting flesh!" Timothy said.

"That's precisely what it is," Klaus said.

They arrived at the first corner and stopped. Klaus inched forward and looked around the passage wall. He saw a small cavern which was empty except for scattered bones of humans and animals strewn across the cavern floor.

"Nice!" Timothy said, moving up beside him to gaze with horror-filled eyes into the small cavern.

Gloria appeared beside Timothy and gasped as she stared down at the scattered bones.

"This way," Klaus whispered.

They crossed the small cavern and came to two passages on the other side. Klaus pointed to the passage on the left and walked towards it.

"Are you sure this is the right one?"

Timothy asked.

"I'm sure," Klaus said, entering the passage which was smaller than the previous passage they had taken. Both Gloria and Timothy entered the passage behind him and followed him along it trying to be as quiet as possible. Once again, burning torches were fixed to the walls on either side at various intervals. After some minutes, the passage turned and came to an opening. Beyond them, they could see another cavern, but unlike the first one they had come to, this one was huge. Light from fires down below flicked on the cavern walls. Klaus lay down and gestured for both Gloria and Timothy to do the same, and together, they crawled forward to the edge of a ledge and looked down into the huge cavern below. There, beneath them, they saw saw about thirty zombies, some of whom were sitting around a fire which had been built in the cavern's centre. The smoke from the fire rose upward towards the cavern's high roof and exited through a hole which was obviously used as a chimney leading up to the surface. Some of the other zombies were lying on the cavern floor, others were sitting in small groups and a few were fighting among themselves. The tall zombie with the bright green eyes, whom Timothy had seen before, sat eating meat and sucking at the bones, his mouth and body covered with blood.

"That's my uncle," Klaus whispered, pointing down to the green-eyed zombie. "He's their leader."

Timothy looked around trying to see Jenny, and then he saw her.

"There's Jenny!" Timothy whispered, pointing down at her.

Jenny was sitting not far away from Klaus' uncle. She seemed to be arguing about a piece of meat with another zombie, each of them pulling at the meat that each had hold of. Timothy stared at her in horror as he noticed her pale white face and the scab-like skin which had transformed her once pretty face into ghoulish monster-like features.

"She ... she's changed!" Timothy whispered, almost to himself.

"What did you expect?" Gloria said, looking at him. "Did you expect to find her the same as she was before?"

Tears formed in Timothy's eyes as he stared silently down at Jenny, his girlfriend who had been transformed into a monster, a zombie.

"There ... there must be something we can do!" he whispered. "Something ... anything!"

Klaus looked at him, "Do you still want to rescue her?" he asked.

Timothy remained silent, staring down at Jenny as if he could not believe that it was really her.

"Timothy?" Gloria said, studying him. "Do you still want to rescue her?"

Timothy continued to remain silent, then, after a moment, he nodded.

"Maybe … maybe there's some way to help her."

"He turned to Klaus, "There must be some way, right?"

Klaus saw the sadness and desperation in Timothy's face as he asked the question.

Klaus paused, then he nodded, "Maybe … " he said, "maybe there's a way."

Timothy looked back down at Jenny who had now finished her argument with the other zombie over the meat and was now walking with jerky steps towards Klaus' green-eyed uncle. Timothy gasped in shock as Jenny knelt down in front of the zombie leader, placed her arms around him and kissed him. Timothy spun round to lie on his back, unable to stand seeing Jenny kiss the green-eyed zombie.

"No!" he breathed to himself, staring upwards with tear-filled eyes.

"No!' he repeated, now squeezing his eyes tightly shut.

Gloria studied him for a moment, then looked at Klaus.

"How do you want to do this?" she asked. "There are too many of them to just go down there."

Klaus nodded, "We need a diversion, something to draw them away."

He knelt up, "I guess this is going to have to be me," he said.

"What?" Gloria said, surprised at his idea.

"Like I said, the vampires and the zombies have a truce. If they see a vampire here, on their territory, they'll go after him and try to kill him."

"I thought green-eyes there was your uncle," Gloria said.

Klaus looked down at his uncle who now had his arms around Jenny.

"He's a zombie," Klaus said. "He's lost any feelings he had, he has no feelings for me."

Klaus sighed sadly, then looked at Gloria, "As soon as they begin to chase me, get down there and save the girl."

Gloria gazed into his eyes.

"You're taking a great risk." she said.

Klaus shrugged," What would you care if they killed another vampire, right?"

Gloria stared at him in silence.

"Go get the girl!" Klaus said, then turned, moved back from the ledge, and went into the passage behind them.

# PART 29

Both Gloria and Timothy looked down at the large cavern below them from the edge of the ledge where they lay. Suddenly, to the right, they saw Klaus enter the cavern from a passage. He was holding his sword ready to strike the first zombie who ran towards him. The noise the zombies were making in the cavern below stopped as every zombie turned to stare towards him. There was a moment of surprised silence, then every zombie began growling loudly and rose to their feet.

"Zombie pigs!" Klaus shouted, his voice echoing around the cavern.

One of the zombies nearby leapt towards him growling savagely. Klaus stood firmly with his sword ready and swung his sword in an arc chopping off the zombie's head with one stroke as the zombie reached him. The zombie's head fell to the floor rolling to the left. The other zombies growled wildly and started running towards him. Klaus turned and ran back into the passage followed by the large pack of angry growling zombies. Green Eyes was one of the first zombies to run into the passage after him leaving Jenny to sit by herself and watch. Only a handful of zombies now remained in the cavern. Jenny looked round and quickly got up to run across the cavern floor to a large piece of meat that one of the other zombies had been eating and had left behind.

"Let's go," Gloria whispered to Timothy.

Timothy followed as Gloria moved along the ledge to the right towards another ledge which led down to the cavern below. Timothy glanced down at Jenny as he made his way down and saw that she was now eating the meat greedily as if she were some kind of wild animal. As they almost reached the bottom, one of the zombies glanced up and saw them. It growled ferociously making the other zombies look up. Gloria jumped down from the last remaining feet of the ledge and ran towards them raising her sword to strike as she went. Timothy jumped down behind her and followed her at a run across the cavern floor brandishing his sword in both hands, gripping it tightly. Gloria managed to chop the head off the first zombie who attacked her, she avoided another, kicking him aside, and chopped the head off a third zombie. Timothy ran over towards Jenny. A zombie ran towards him but instead of trying to chop its head off, Timothy plunged the sword straight into its chest. The zombie growled and reached towards him with its clawed fingers on both hands. Quickly, Timothy pulled the blade out of its body, stepped back and swung the sword at the zombie's neck. The zombie's head came off and fell to the floor rolling away from him. He turned, saw another zombie growling and coming towards him, and this time immediately aimed his sword for the zombie's neck. The head fell from the zombie and the headless zombie's body fell to its knees, a thick green liquid spewing out of its neck and onto the ground around it. Timothy turned and saw Gloria doing the same to another zombie. Suddenly, he saw Jenny growling wildly and running towards him.

"Jenny!" he called. "Jenny! It's me!"

But Jenny didn't stop and leapt up at him knocking him down onto his back. Jenny growled above him, clawing at him and lowering her head to bite him.

"Jenny!" Timothy shouted, trying to push her off.

The next instant, Jenny stopped growling and fell over him uncon-scious. Timothy looked up and saw Gloria standing above him. She had hit Jenny on the back of the head with the handle of her sword.

"Nice girlfriend you have!" Gloria said, looking down at him. "I don't think she was trying to kiss you!"

Timothy pushed Jenny to one side and stood up staring down at her.

"Thanks!" he said to Gloria. "Thank you!"

Gloria looked round at the headless dead zombies now strewn across the cavern floor.

"We'd better go before they come back!" she said.

Timothy nodded, knelt down, picked Jenny up, and placed her over his shoulder. He followed Gloria as she led the way across the cavern floor to the ledge leading up to the passage through which they had come.

# PART 30

Klaus stopped running through the passage and turned. The passage he had taken below was just wide enough for him to swing his sword. He beheaded the first zombie who approached him growling savagely, and then the second. He kicked at the third knocking the zombie back into the others behind him, then he turned and ran further along the passage. After some minutes, he could feel a breeze coming from somewhere up ahead and knew that he was near the exit. As the zombies continue to growl, running after him further back along the passage, he came to two separate passages, one branching to the left, and the other branching to the right. He took the passage to the right, feeling the breeze coming from it and ran along it as fast as he could. He felt the cool breeze air coming faster now and as he turned a corner in the passage he heard a cry, and in the light from one of the flickering wall torches, he saw the blade of a sword aimed towards his neck. Gloria stopped herself from cutting off his head just in time. Klaus stared at her as she lowered her weapon.

"The girl?" he asked.

Gloria gestured behind her.

"We got her," she said.

Klaus looked behind her and saw Timothy carrying Jenny over his shoulder. The growling of the approaching zombies grew louder from the passage behind Klaus.

"Go!" Klaus shouted. "They're just behind!"

He pushed Gloria forward and she followed behind Timothy as he turned to move along the passage which was now leading upwards to the exit. Timothy's feet slipped on the slope as he went, but finally he reached the top and stepped out to breathe the fresh air. Gloria followed him out, then came Klaus who was looking behind him, ready to behead any zombie who came out of the hole after them.

"Go! Go! Go!" Gloria shouted, pushing Timothy on up the slope towards the trees above. They climbed up the slope as fast as possible, neither Timothy nor Gloria daring to glance back as they did so. Klaus made his way up the slope behind them, glancing back from time to time. At last, they reached the top and ran through the trees of the forest. A zombie came growling out of the darkness to their left. Klaus quickly ran towards it, avoiding its claws, and swung his sword to behead it. Another zombie appeared, and this time it was Gloria who had to avoid its claws. She managed to step back and swing her sword, swinging it with a force to cut off its head. Timothy kept running through the trees as fast as he could as he carried Jenny on his shoulder hearing the growling zombies coming from somewhere behind in the darkness. He ran on, unconscious of time, with only one thought on his mind, save Jenny, save Jenny! Finally, he entered the clearing and saw the strange orange glowing triangular ship up ahead in front of him.

"Julia! Julia!" Timothy shouted as he neared it. "Open the door! Open the door!"

He glanced round expecting to see a zombie coming up behind him, but he saw Gloria and Klaus. The door suddenly slid open and Timothy ran inside followed by Gloria, but Klaus turned, saw two zombies closing in on him and ran at them with his sword raised. He beheaded the first, turned and beheaded the second, and then saw a third, a fourth and a fifth zombie running towards him. Klaus turned, ran for the triangular ship and jumped inside just before the door slid shut behind him. He dropped his sword to the floor and breathed a sigh of relief as the zombies outside now began to bang at the ship's door. He remained still, listening to the growling and the banging of the zombies outside, as he stared across at Timothy who was now lying Jenny gently down onto the ship's wide sofa-like seat. Suddenly, he noticed the young oriental girl standing next to the ship's console and staring across at him. Yuki stood completely still, staring fixedly into Klaus' eyes.

"Like I said," Julia said, standing beside her, "don't worry, he's ... not like the others."

Gloria dropped her sword moving over towards Yuki.

"How do you feel?" Gloria asked, with concern in her voice, touching Yuki's arm gently.

Yuki remained silent, staring at Klaus, then she placed her head to one side.

"You are right," she said to Julia. "He is not like the others, I feel it."

Julia glanced at Gloria, "She ... she seems to be able to feel things. She says that this ship talks to her."

Yuki turned to Julia, "It does! It ... it tells me that it is not happy!"

Both Julia and Gloria glanced at each other strangely.

Yuki turned to look down at Jenny.

"A zombie!" she said.

Timothy glanced up at her, a displeased expression on his face.

Klaus moved over to the ship's controls.

"We should leave," he said, observing the controls on the circular console.

"Any idea where we'll go?" Gloria asked, looking at him.

Klaus shook his head, studying the controls in front of him, "Like I said, this ship wasn't finished, we could end up anywhere."

Yuki moved forward to stand beside him.

"The blue buttons," she said. "Press the blue buttons, then pull this lever," she said, pointing at the lever on the console to her right.

"How ... would you know?" Klaus asked, looking ot her.

Yuki shrugged, "Like I said, this ship talks to me."

Without another word, Yuki reached forward, pressed the blue buttons and pulled the lever.

Suddenly, the ship started to vibrate.

"What did you do?" Julia shouted, gazing around wide-eyed as the ship's vibrations grew stronger.

A moment later, a loud whirring machine-like noise began to sound. Coloured lights flashed on the console. Julia screamed, holding onto the console to steady herself.

"The screen!" Gloria shouted, pointing up to the screen on the wall.

Each of them looked up at the screen. It now showed nothing, only a blackness as if they were now nowhere, absolutely nowhere at all.

# PART 31

THE VIBRATIONS AND THE LOUD WHIRRING SOUND OF THE MACHINE STOPPED. EACH OF THEM STARED UP AT THE SCREEN. ONLY YUKI SEEMED CALM AND STARED UP AT THE SCREEN WITH A SMILE ON HER FACE. SUDDENLY, AN IMAGE APPEARED. IT WAS DAYTIME OUTSIDE THE SHIP, AND ALTHOUGH IT APPEARED THAT THEY WERE STILL IN THE FOREST, THEY WERE LOOKING AT A STRANGE ANGULAR SHAPED RED BUILDING THAT ROSE ABOVE THE TREETOPS FAR BEYOND ON THE OTHER SIDE OF A FIELD.

"WHERE THE HELL ARE WE?" GLORIA SAID TO HERSELF, STARING UP AT THE STRANGE LOOKING BUILDING ON THE SCREEN.

"WELL, I GUESS WE'VE GOT TO LOOK AT THE BRIGHT SIDE," JULIA SAID. "AT LEAST, WE'RE AWAY FROM THE ZOMBIES!"

Each of the others looked at her.

"Have you ever heard of the expression, out of the frying pan and into the fire?" Gloria asked.

"We don't know where we are," Klaus said, staring up at the screen. "We could be anywhere."

"Well, that's an understatement," Gloria said, under her breath.

"We're where we need to be," Yuki said, gazing up at the screen.

The others looked at her.

"What the hell does that mean?" Julia asked. "Do you know something we don't?"

Yuki turned to her, "I don't," she said, "but the ship does."

"Do you mean ... " Gloria said, "the ship ...

wanted us to come here?"

"Why?" Julia asked. "Where are we? Why are we here?"

Yuki remained calm as she smiled at her, "I don't know," she said. "But the ship knows."

Each of them stared at her, then Klaus went over to Timothy and looked down at Jenny who was still lying on the sofa-like seat unconscious.

"We should tie her up," he said.

Gloria nodded behind him, "I agree," she said.

Timothy looked at them both. He remained silent for a moment, then nodded, "Okay, but I'll do it."

"I'll get you something," Klaus said, turning to walk over to the sliding panel in the wall on the other side of the ship. He found a cable and came back over to hand it to Timothy. Timothy paused staring down at Jenny, then began to tie up her wrists and ankles.

"I GUESS IF WE'RE HERE," GLORIA SAID, LOOKING AT YUKI, "IT'S NOT JUST TO HANG AROUND INSIDE THE SHIP, RIGHT? WE'RE SUPPOSED TO GO OUTSIDE?" SHE GLANCED UP AT IMAGE OF THE BUILDING ON THE SCREEN. "IS THAT WHERE WE HAVE TO GO?"

YUKI STARED PAST HER AS IF SHE WERE GAZING INTO SPACE. SHE TURNED HER HEAD TO THE SIDE SEEMING TO BE LISTENING TO SOMETHING, OR SOMEONE.

"THE BUILDING," SHE SAID, FINALLY, WITH A NOD.

GLORIA NODDED, "THE BUILDING," SHE SAID. "THAT'S WHAT I THOUGHT."

KLAUS WENT BACK OVER TO THEM STARING UP AT THE SCREEN.

"I CAN'T GO," HE SAID. "IT'S SUNNY OUTSIDE, AND ACCORDING TO THESE INSTRUMENTS, IT'S HOT. I'D FRY OUTSIDE, TURN TO DUST."

GLORIA STUDIED HIM, THEN NODDED UNDERSTANDINGLY. SHE TURNED TOWARDS TIMOTHY, "HEY, TIMOTHY!" SHE CALLED. "COMING FOR A WALK?"

Timothy glanced up, "I ... I have to stay here ... with Jenny," he said.

"Look, you can't do anything for her right now," Gloria said. "We have to go find out where we are. Maybe we can find some way to help her."

Timothy stared down at Jenny for a moment, then he stood up.

He sighed, "Okay," he said.

He picked up the sword he'd used on the zombies, "I'm taking this," he said.

"Good idea," Gloria agreed, picking up her own sword.

"Do you ... do you want me to go with you?" Julia asked, with a worried tone to her voice.

Gloria looked at her and smiled, "No, it's okay Julia, you can stay here."

JULIA GLANCED WITH WORRIED LOOKING EYES AT KLAUS, JENNY AND AT YUKI.

"WITH A VAMPIRE? A ZOMBIE? AND A ... A WEIRD PERSON?" SHE SAID, STARING AT YUKI.

GLORIA SHRUGGED, "WELL, YOU'RE WELCOME TO COME IF YOU ... "

JULIA NODDED, "GREAT!" SHE SAID, GOING OVER TO PICK UP KLAUS' SWORD WHERE HE HAD DROPPED IT.

KLAUS MOVED TO THE CONSOLE TO PRESS THE SWITCH TO OPEN THE DOOR, BUT YUKI BEAT HIM TO IT. THE DOOR SLID OPEN. KLAUS LOOKED AT HER, "HOW DID YOU KNOW ... ?"

YUKI SHRUGGED, "LIKE I SAID, THE SHIP TELLS ME THINGS."

GLORIA TOOK A DEEP BREATH LOOKING OUTSIDE THE SHIP'S OPEN DOOR.

"OKAY," SHE SAID, TURNING TO BOTH TIMOTHY AND JULIA, "LET'S GO!"

THE THREE OF THEM STEPPED OUTSIDE INTO THE BRIGHT SUNLIGHT SHADING THEIR EYES, THEIR SWORDS GLINTING IN THE LIGHT AS THEY WENT.

# PART 32

The sunlight seemed much brighter than usual as they walked through the forest. They noticed flowers that they'd never seen before and the air smelled sweet from their fragrance.

Timothy stopped to study a purple flower with pink edges. He reached out to touch it and it moved. Timothy froze, staring down at the flower curiously.

"Hey!" Gloria called out, glancing back to him. "You'd better keep up with us! You don't want to get lost!"

Timothy looked up, "Coming!" he called.

He glanced back down at the flower once more, then turned to continue, following both Gloria and Julia though the forest.

"Wow!" Julia exclaimed, as they came out of the forest and stood in a clearing gazing up at the huge red and very strange looking building.

"I've never seen a building like that before!" Julia said, staring up at the building in awe.

"Neither have I," Gloria said, standing beside her.

"What do you think it is?" Timothy said, also staring up at the building.

"Don't know," Gloria said, "but it's something."

"It's right in the middle of nowhere!" Julia said, gazing around at the large clearing in the forest in which they stood.

"Do you ... do you think we've travelled back in time?" she asked.

Timothy looked at her, "Do you see that building?" he said, pointing at the strange red building in front of them. "I'd say we went forward into the future!"

Gloria glanced at him, "Let's hope you're wrong," she said.

They moved forward, heading across the clearing towards the other end and the strange huge red building which towered up to the sky on the other side. The building rose high above them as they reached its doors. There were two large doors, one of which stood slightly open. Timothy pushed it forward opening it some more. The door creaked in the surrounding silence as it slowly opened. Gloria glanced at her two companions, then stepped forward and went inside. The others followed through the opening and then stopped to look at the huge hall in which they now found themselves. The hall was empty except for a white circular desk which stood in its centre with various comfortable looking seats behind it.

"It looks like nobody's home," Gloria said, gazing around as the three of them walked towards the desk.

"What's that?" Timothy asked, pointing to a small black box on the desk.

"Maybe it's some kind of intercom," Julia said.

She reached over the desk and pressed a button, but nothing happened.

All three of them stood looking around at the huge empty hall.

"Spooky," Julia said.

Timothy glanced at her and smiled, "I thought the castle was spookier," he said.

"Hey, just a thought," Julia said, looking at him.

"You're right," Gloria said to Timothy. "It was a spooky old castle. They used oil lamps and candles, no electricity, so ... where did Klaus' father get the equipment to build a sophisticated Time Machine?"

Both Timothy and Julia stared at her.

"Good point," Timothy said. "If it really is a Time Machine."

"Well, maybe we can ask Klaus when we get back," Julia said, glancing round at the hall.

"I say we split up," Timothy said. "Meet back here in, say, thirty minutes."

"I don't have a watch," Julia said.

Timothy took the watch off his wrist and handed it to her.

"Here," he said. "Take mine, I have a good sense of time."

"I'll take the right side," Gloria said, turning to walk towards a passage leading off the hall to the right.

"I'm left," Timothy said, walking away to the left.

"Hey!" Julia called out. "Where do I go?"

Timothy turned back to her with a smile, "You're a big girl, you figure it out!"

Julia pouted, watching him walk away.

"Thanks a lot!" she said to herself, looking around the hall to see if there was another place to go.

Gloria found a lift. She stepped inside looking at the buttons for all of the floors, then pressed the top button. The lift doors slid silently closed and then the lift sped up towards the top floor so fast that it made her ears pop. Within seconds, the lift had reached the top floor. The lift bell rang, and the doors slid open. Gloria stepped out, raising her sword, ready to hit anyone with it if necessary. The corridor in which she found herself looked empty. She relaxed and walked along it looking in all of the rooms as she went. Some rooms were empty, but other rooms had strangely shaped desks and chairs with large screens on the walls. She looked around these rooms but found nothing of interest and continued on along the corridor. Finally she came to a hall with a large circular desk running around it. There were various seats around the desk, and in front of each seat there was a screen. Gloria sat down in one of the seats and tried to work the screen in front of her. There were strange switches and different coloured buttons, but whatever Gloria did, nothing seemed to turn on the screen. Finally, she ended up hitting it with her hand. Suddenly, she heard a noise. She froze. It had come from the corridor leading off to the right. Slowly, she reached down for the sword she'd leaned against the desk beside her. She stood up quietly, then walked across the hall towards the corridor on the right and stood against the wall, gripping the sword tightly in her hands and listening. She heard footsteps coming slowly along the corridor towards her. Holding her breath, she waited, ready to strike whoever it was with the sword.

# PART 33

The footsteps came closer.

Suddenly Gloria cried out turning the corner and raising the sword in her hands ready to strike.

Timothy jumped back with a cry, staring at the sword raise towards him with wide eyes.

"Timothy!" Gloria said in surprise, lowering her sword.

Timothy breathed a sigh of relief and leaned back against the corridor wall.

"It looks like we had the same idea," Gloria said, "to come to the top floor."

Timothy nodded, "I did go to a floor below at first," he said, "but it was empty, so I came up to the top."

"Come and look at this," Gloria said, turning back to the hall.

She led Timothy back over to the large circular desk with the various seats and screens. She sat down in one of the seats and tried unsuccessfully to turn it on.

"Any ideas how to turn it on?" she asked, glancing at him. "Maybe there's something important on it."

She looked back to the blank screen, "If only we could get it to work!"

Timothy leaned forward, studying the screen and the various switches and buttons. He tried a few but nothing happened. Finally, he shook his head, "No idea," he said. "Maybe it works with a fingerprint, or a voice." He looked around at the hall, "I didn't find anything, just empty rooms, a few desks here and there, nothing much."

"Me too," Gloria said, studying the screen in front of her curiously.

Timothy noticed two large doors to his right at the far end of the hall. He walked over to them, studied them for a moment, then slid them apart. They opened up to show some kind of platform beyond a wide floor. The platform was semi-circular and in front of it was a huge window stretching the whole length of the semi-circular platform from the ceiling down to the floor. Timothy walked through the open doors, across the floor and onto the platform, and stood gazing down at the view in front of him. The view was breathtaking. He looked down over the forest. There were fields, lakes and rolling hills, but he saw no sign of any other buildings, no towns, no cities, just the forest and wild countryside stretching far towards the horizon. The sun was beginning to set, and red, pink and purple colours filled the sky.

Suddenly, he noticed something.

He took a step forward staring at what he had noticed. His mouth opened in surprise. Gloria was still trying to get the screen on the circular desk in front of her to work when Timothy came running back into the hall.

"Gloria! Gloria!" he called urgently. "You have to see this!"

Gloria looked up at him

"What is it?" she asked.

"It ... it's the moon!" Timothy said.

Gloria stared at him,"The moon?" she repeated. "What about the moon?"

"Just come and have a look!" Timothy said urgently.

Gloria stood up and walked across the hall to the two large sliding doors. She followed Timothy through them and onto the platform inside the wide room.

"Nice view!" she said, gazing down at the wooded landscape far below.

"Look!" Timothy said, pointing up at the sky.

Gloria looked up and saw the moon, but what she saw next surprised her. Instead of only one moon, there were two.

"Remember what I said about we may have gone into the future?" Timothy said.

Gloria remained silent, staring up at the two large moons in the sky above them.

"Well, I was wrong," Timothy continued. "I think we're on another planet!"

# PART 34

Julia, who had decided to look in the basement, now approached two large metal doors at the end of a corridor. She stopped in front of them, staring at them, wondering if they were locked, then she took one step closer and the metal doors slid open. Julia paused before stepping forward, gazing around at the large room beyond the doors. It looked like some kind of laboratory. There were work benches, tables, desks and various strange looking instruments with different coloured chemicals in glass-like containers as if someone had been conducting some kind of experiment. Julia moved slowly forward, looking around as she went. There was a humming noise of electricity from the lights overhead. She saw screens, machines, and what looked like a sophisticated looking computers on both sides of the large room. As she walked, something cracked under her left foot and she looked down. It was one of the glass-like containers which had fallen to the floor and lay broken. Around her, on the floor, she saw other glass-like containers which also lay broken on the floor. It looked like someone, or something, had been throwing things to the floor in a rage. She walked carefully forward, the glass-like containers cracking under her feet as she went. Apart from the cracking noise as Julia moved forward, and the low humming noise of electricity, the large lab-like room was completely silent.

Suddenly, she heard a noise and jerked around. She paused, listening. For a moment, she heard nothing, apart from the humming of the electricity, then she heard the noise again. She turned towards it. It had come from her left. She saw a closed door on the other side of the large room and walked towards it, raising her sword in both hands as she went. The noise came again as she stopped in front of the door. She stood listening, studying the door in front of her. The was no handle, nor any button on the wall next to it with which to open it. She reached out a hand and touched the wall beside the door, feeling around it, searching for something that would open it. And then she found it. She could barely see it, it was a small circular pad which seemed to be part of the wall. Julia hesitated for a moment, then pressed it. There was another low humming sound, then the door slid open. She raised her sword ready to strike, then stepped forward into the smaller room. She heard someone crying from somewhere inside and stopped. She remained still, listening and gripping the handle of the sword tightly in both hands. Carefully, she looked around the room. It seemed to be some kind of store room with various metal boxes piled up here and there, and shelves with different kinds of strange looking instruments on them. Julia advanced forward some more, and then she saw him.

Behind one of the metal boxes was a man, possibly in his fifties, he was sitting on the floor, visibly shaking and staring up at her with wide fearful eyes.

"D ... don't hurt me!" the man said, raising his hands in front of him. "P ... please!"

Julia stared down at him, her mouth gaping open in surprise. She noticed that the man was staring at the sword in her hands. Slowly, she placed it to one side, leaning it against one of the metal boxes. Julia crouched down in front of him and reached out to take his shaking hands in hers.

She gave him a smile, "It's okay, you're safe … you're safe," she said.


Both Gloria and Timothy reached the building's entrance hall on the ground floor and stood waiting in front of the desk.

"Where is she?" Timothy said, glancing around.

"She must have lost track of time," Gloria said.

"With my watch?" Timothy said.

He looked out through the open door of the building's entrance, "It's getting dark," he said.

"Why are we here?" Gloria said, gazing around at the building's huge hall in which they stood.

"What do you mean?" Timothy asked.

"I mean … why are we here? This place? Klaus told us that his father was building a Time Machine so that he could go back and change the past, only … we didn't travel back in time, we travelled through space … to this planet."

"You think … Klaus' father wasn't building a Time Machine, but … a Spaceship?" Timothy asked.

Gloria looked around, shaking her head, "I don't know," she said. "But it's not a conventional Spaceship. You see how fast it took us to get here?"

"Minutes," Timothy said.

Gloria glanced at him, "More like seconds," she said. "Do you remember what Yuki said? she said, we're where we are meant to be. What did she mean by that?"

Timothy shrugged, "She seems to have some kind of communication with the ship," he said.

"A ship that thinks?" Gloria said, looking at him. "That can communicate?"

"Apparently only with Yuki," Timothy said. "She seems to have gift of some kind."

"If only we knew where 'here' was," Gloria said, "maybe we'd ... "

Suddenly, Julia emerged from the other side of the huge hall walking towards them, but she wasn't alone. There was a man walking beside her, an older man, possibly in his fifties, with long white wiry hair and wearing strange clothes. As he approached, they could see that he was walking shakily, gazing around with wide eyes as if he were in fear of something.

Both Gloria and Timothy stared at him as he walked beside Julia over to them.

"This is Sharn," Julia said, gesturing towards the strange looking man. "He was hiding in the basement."

Gloria, staring at the man in surprise, stepped in front of him.

"Who are you?" she asked. "What is this place? Where are we?"

Sharn looked at her, then turned his head and noticed that one of the doors to the main entrance was open. He stared through the open door at the approaching darkness of the night, then gasped as if he were in shock and immediately ran over to the open door to close it.

"What's he doing?" Timothy asked, watching him.

"He's afraid," Julia said, from behind them. Both Gloria and Timothy turned to face her.

"He's been hiding," Julia said. "Since they stormed the building, attacking them."

"Since ... who stormed the building?" Timothy asked.

"Zombies," Julia said. "Apparently, this building is in no man's land between zombie territory and vampire territory, but slightly closer to zombie territory."

Both Gloria and Timothy stared at her, then jerked quickly around as they heard Sharn close the building's main entrance door behind them.

"Then ... that explains it," Gloria said. "We're on the planet where Klaus' father, and his uncle, were ... infected. We're on a planet completely overrun with zombies and vampires!"

"And it's getting dark," Julia said.

# PART 35

They sat in the hall on the top floor around the large circular desk.

"I'm a scientist," Sharn said. "Just like Erik Stolz and his brother, Delph, were hundreds of years ago."

"They're still alive," Gloria said, studying Sharn carefully.

"I don't doubt it," Sharn said. "From what we've learned about these ... creatures, they seem to have a much longer life span. They seem to be able to stay young, or ... to regenerate, by drinking the blood of others, particularly a human species like yours and mine. Erik was, maybe still is, a genius. After what happened to him, his brother and their crew we decided to come here and study the two species, the vampires and the zombies as you call them. We built this building in no man's land, between the two warring sides, and worked here, in what we thought was a safe place. It was supposed to be a fortress, keeping the creatures out. Here, we studied some of the creatures whom we captured during the daytime, when they were most vulnerable. We knew where they slept. Unfortunately, some of our team members became infected, and this is what happened. The infected members opened the doors at night, and the creatures from outside swarmed in. The people here were ... massacred, killed horribly. I ... I heard screams ... terrible, horrible screams! ... The next spaceship coming from my own planet with supplies wasn't due for another six months, so I hid. I ... I thought I would die."

"What kind of experiments were you doing on these creatures?" Gloria asked.

Sharn sighed, gazing down sadly, "We knew that Erik, his brother, and the other members of their team would survive. We knew that if we could find a cure, we could help them. We sent them on a spaceship to the nearest planet, your planet, Earth. The ship crashed into a lake. It was designed to send out a large invisible force field to cover a large area, imprisoning only those who are infected in the the area of the crash. The villagers nearby tried to escape, but the vampires, Erik and his people, captured their families and kept them prisoner, forcing the people in the village to stay and work for them. The villagers, of course, were not affected by the force field and could leave, but if they did so, their families would die, so they were forced to help the vampires. The villagers could go out of the forest, beyond the force field, and bring back whatever the vampires asked for, sometimes even humans. The vampires forbade them from using modern things and kept them living in the old ways. They were afraid that with new technology, the villagers would find a way to beat them."

"How do you know all this?" Timothy asked.

"Because ... " Sharn said, "I was a member of a team that went to Earth to check up on them, to see if they were still alive, to see if they had changed somehow. The zombies, who were more like wild animals than anything else, almost captured us, but Erik and his friends saved us. He knew we had come from his home planet to visit his prison to check up on them. He asked us to give him some material, he said that he wanted to build a Time Machine to go back in time and change the past, change what had happened to him and his team. We told him that we were working on an antidote for their infection, but he said that if he could go back in the past, everything would be made right. Seeing as how he was such a brilliant scientist, we thought that if anyone could build such a machine and could change the past, he could. But later, we found out what his real intention was, he was neither interested in the antidote, nor in going back to the past to change what had happened, both he and his team had changed completely. Erik, did not want to stop being a vampire, but we found out too late. Instead of a Time Machine, he was using the material we gave him to build a Spaceship, but not like a normal Spaceship, one that could travel in an instant to another planet. He had set the controls to return here, to kill us all and destroy our experiments which could help him and the others who were infected to become normal again. We believe that he wanted to come here and take control of the other vampires on this planet and then spread the infection to other planets, to other universes. They would no longer be imprisoned on the Earth, they would be free to travel anywhere they wanted, and they would have an army. But ... he never came. We believe that his infection stopped him, that somehow it overtook his brain and he couldn't complete the Spaceship, but now ... you are here."

"Which means that he did complete it," Gloria said.

Sharn nodded, "And that is dangerous," he said. "If his infection has made him forget ... and one day, he remembers ..."

Gloria, Timothy and Julia stared at him, waiting in the following silence for Sharn to finish his sentence, "... all life will be at risk." Sharn said finally. "He must be killed."

Suddenly Julia jerked round hearing a noise.

"What is it?" Timothy asked.

They watched as Julia stood up and ran

across the hall to the open sliding doors and went out onto the viewing platform.

She gazed down through the large semi-circular windows. It was night time, but beneath the light of the two moons which hung in the sky above she could easily see the horde of zombies moving closer below towards the building.

Julia looked back towards the others who were coming out onto the platform to join her.

"We've got company!" Julia said.

# PART 36

They watched as the zombies reached the building and began banging on the doors, growling like wild beasts.

"Can they get in?" Gloria asked Sharn.

"Before, I would have said no," Sharn replied. "But now, I'm not sure."

Timothy looked at him, "You said you were working on an antidote for the infected, how far did you get?"

Sharn sighed, "We were still experimenting with it. I believe we made a breakthrough, but ... we weren't sure about side effects, we had no time to complete our research."

"The antidote for vampires, is it the same antidote for the zombies?" Timothy asked.

"With a slight variation," Sharn said, "it should be almost the same. Of course, it would only work on those who have been changed, not those born with the infection."

Julia looked at Gloria, "Like Klaus," she said.

"My ... my girlfriend," Timothy said to Sharn, "she ... she was changed, into a ... a zombie. Will it ... work on her?"

Sharn studied him for a moment, then nodded, "It may do," he said. "Like I said, we weren't able to complete our tests.

Timothy grabbed Sharn's arm, "How long?" he asked, squeezing Sharn's arm tightly as he spoke. "How long will it take to ... to cure her?"

"I ... I'm not sure," Sharn said, staring wide-eyed at Timothy, obviously shaken by Timothy's tight grip on his arm. "It ... it depends on how long they have been infected. If it's less than twenty-four hours, it should be fast, may ... maybe two hours, maybe less, any longer and I can't be sure. In fact, any longer and I'm not really sure that it will work at all, that ... that's what we were working on, we ... we wanted to cure everyone, especially long term cases like Erik."

Timothy glanced at Gloria.

"We can save her!" he said. "It's been less than twenty-four hours!"

Sharn looked at them both.

"Do you have the antidote?" Julia asked, looking at Sharn.

Sharn turned to her, then nodded, "Y ... yes! Yes! It's in the lab, downstairs!"

"Come on! Let's go!" Timothy said, now pulling Sharn back towards the open sliding doors.

Gloria grabbed Timothy's arm, "What are you going to do?" she asked. "If you get it, you can't go out there at night! We have to wait until morning!"

Timothy pulled free from Gloria's arm, "I can't wait!" he said. "You heard what he said! We have more chance of curing her if it's been less than twenty-four hours! The longer we wait, the less chance she has! We have to go now!"

"Have you seen how many zombies there are outside the building?" Gloria asked.

"This is my girlfriend we're talking about!" Timothy shouted.

"Timothy," Gloria said, "You're not thinking clearly, it's suicide to to out there right now!"

"Then don't go! Stay here! But 1 can't wait! I ... I can't!"

Timothy turned back to Sharn and pushed him forward, "Let's go! You're going to get that antidote for me!"

"Timothy!" Julia said, pointing to Gloria. "She's right! You know she's right! It's suicide to go out there right now!"

Sharn looked at the three of them.

"We ... we have weapons," he said.

He glanced at their swords, "Modern weapons," he added.

# PART 37

Back in the basement lab, Sharn touched a hidden pad on the wall and part of the wall beside it slid open. Both Gloria and Julia stared at the amount of strange looking weapons and other objects which filled the large cupboard.

Laser guns," Sharn said, handing them both two laser guns which looked like large futuristic rifles.

"What's this?" Gloria asked, picking up a small circular disc.

"That's a grenade," Sharn said.

Gloria took a few, handed a grenade to Julia, and then looked at him,

"Why didn't you use these?" Gloria asked, picking up a bag and putting various weapons into it.

"Didn't have time!" Sharn said, taking a laser gun for himself.

Timothy, who was studying a chemical work bench not far away, turned to look at him.

"Are you sure this antidote will work?" he asked, holding up a glass-like vial with green liquid inside.

Sharn stared at him for a moment, "I ... I promise nothing," he said. "But we can try."

Timothy stared back at him, then nodded. He put the vial filled with the liquid in his pocket together with a clean syringe-like object wrapped in a material similar to plastic, then he went over to the large cupboard and picked up one of the laser guns.

"Aim for their necks," Sharn said, looking at Gloria and the others.

"We know," Gloria said.

"I'm aiming for anything I can!" Timothy said.

Gloria looked at him, "Just aim for the necks," she said. She glanced at the others, "Are you ready?" she asked.

Julia nodded, but Sharn seemed undecided.

Gloria studied him and saw the fear in his eyes.

"I ... I'm a scientist," he said. "I'm ... not used to ..."

"It's kill or be killed," Gloria said, staring at him.

Sharn remained silent for a moment staring back into her eyes, then he lowered his head and nodded, "Okay," he said nervously, "let's ... let's go."

# PART 38

The sound of the banging against the main doors of the building was loud. Gloria and the others stood in front of the closed doors, listening to the banging and the animal-like growling sounds of the zombies on the other side of them. Gloria turned and nodded to Sharn who was standing near the wall beside the large metal doors.

"Open them," She said.

Sharn paused, then reached out his hand to press the wall pad as each of the others raised their weapons ready to fire.

"D ... don't forget," Sharn said, "aim for the neck."

He pressed the wall pad and the doors started to open. Gloria quickly threw a small metal disc grenade through the gap between the doors before they were completely open. They heard an explosion outside and cries from the zombies, and then the doors were fully open. Gloria and the others fired their weapons at the zombies who were left near the doors after the explosion, and then Gloria threw another grenade and another explosion sounded accompanied by more cries, and then Gloria, Julia and Timothy ran through the open doors followed by Sharn, each of them firing their laser guns at the remaining zombies as they ran outside. The zombies cried out and growled angrily clawing towards them as the small group ran through them firing their laser guns as they went. They managed to cut a straight path through the zombies, firing their lasers and going as fast as they could as they advanced in tight formation across the clearing in front of the building. They moved in unison, as if they were one unit, until, now running faster and picking up speed, they cleared their way through the surrounding zombies and ran for the trees with the zombies chasing them from behind. Gloria led the others, running though the trees as fast as she could. Julia held back, firing at the zombies behind them, three zombies lost their heads and the others growled angrily running towards her. Julia turned and continued to run through the trees seeing Timothy running up ahead following behind Sharn and Gloria. She ran for some moments before glancing back. She realized that the zombies here on this planet seemed to move faster than those back on Earth. Julia stopped again and threw back a disc-like grenade. The grenade exploded sending zombie body parts flying in all directions. Julia continued on through the trees, this time not daring to look back as she ran. Suddenly, she came out of the trees and entered a clearing to see Gloria, Timothy and Sharn, each standing still and staring in front of them.

"What is it?" Julia asked, running forward, "What's wrong?"

And then, she saw the reason why they had stopped.

There, standing in front of them, on the other side of the small clearing, were about twenty vampires. The lead vampire, who as tall and thin, stepped forward with a fiendish grin on his face, his grin showing his pointed fangs.

"You will die!" The vampire hissed to them, his grin remaining on his face.

Gloria raised her weapon to fire, but when she squeezed the trigger she realized that the weapon was not working. The lead vampire's terrible grin widened. He held up a small box-like gadget in his hand.

"It's a weapon controller!" Sharn said, seeing the object in the vampire's hand. The others remained still, not taking their eyes off the long line of vampires standing in front of them. "They must have taken it when they entered the building! When it's turned on, our weapons won't work in a two-hundred yard radius!"

"How'd they know what it was?" Julia asked from behind him.

Sharn shook his head, "I ... I don't know," he replied, continuing to stare at the vampires.

Each side remained still, staring across at each other. The sound of the growling zombies was now coming closer behind Gloria and the others.

"Any ideas?" Timothy asked, growing even more nervous by the minute.

"Yes," Gloria said suddenly. "Run!"

They ran to the right, following Gloria out of the clearing and back through the trees behind them. The lead vampire howled, running forward, and then the other vampires also ran forward behind him howling loudly as they went. Gloria and the others ran as fast as they could, the branches from trees hitting their faces as they ran, not daring to look back, as the terrible howling of the vampires behind them seemed to be getting closer.

# PART 39

"Got an idea!" Gloria called out as they ran through the trees with the vampires chasing them behind.

"Follow me!"

Gloria ran to the right and the others followed her. The growling of the zombies grew louder as they now seemed to be running directly towards them.

"We're running right back towards the zombies!" Timothy shouted.

"That's the plan!" Gloria shouted to him.

"Are you sure about this?" Julia shouted.

"Trust me!" Gloria shouted back as they ran.

Behind them, Sharn was beginning to wheeze as he tried to keep up with them.

They had almost reached the zombies when Gloria called out again.

"Hard left!" she shouted.

Gloria ran to the left with the others following quickly behind. The vampires, who were chasing them, now found themselves running directly into a large group of growling and angry zombies. The two groups clashed, the vampires howling loudly and the zombies growling fiercely as they began to fight each other.

Gloria and the others continued running, not daring to glance back at the noisy battle which now raged behind them between vampires and zombies. They ran and ran, sometimes stumbling, trying to put as much distance as possible between them and the terrible sounds of the creatures battling farther behind. Finally, when the noise of the battle faded away into the distance, they stopped and fell to their knees, completely exhausted and breathing heavily. Sharn's wheezing had grown worse, he now lay on the ground breathing with difficulty. Gloria pulled herself up onto her feet and went over to him.

"Are you all right?" she asked, kneeling down beside him.

Sharn looked up at her, still wheezing badly, "O ... okay," he managed to reply.

"Those vampires," Gloria said. "They seemed ... quite intelligent."

Sharn managed to lean himself up from the ground, "The ... their leader ..." he said, wheezing as he spoke.

"What about him?" Gloria asked.

"I'm ... not sure, but ... I think he was ... he was one of Erik's team ... called Keno ... he probably ... got left behind."

Gloria nodded, "That would explain it," she said. "If Erik Stolz came back here ..."

"He ... would have ... an army, at his command," Sharn said.

"An army of vampires!" Julia said, coming over to them.

"Exactly," Sharn said, gazing up at her.

"We have to go!" Gloria said, getting up onto her feet.

Both Gloria and Julia helped Sharn up.

Timothy was already standing and gazing around.

"What is it?" Gloria asked, looking at him.

"I ... think I'm lost," he said. "Which way is it?"

Gloria smiled and pointed left towards the trees.

"It's that way!" She said.

"How can you be so sure?" Timothy asked, looking in various directions at the surrounding trees.

"I have a good sense of direction," Gloria said.

She moved forward towards the trees on the left, followed by Sharn.

Both Timothy and Julia looked at each other.

"How does she do that?" Timothy asked.  "All these trees look the same to me."

Julia shrugged, "Don't know, but I'm not going to argue.  Maybe she has a knack or something."

Timothy watched as Julia began to follow after Gloria and Sharn.

"What if that leads us back to them?" he called out.  "The zombies and the vampires!"

He glanced around once more.

"Some knack!" he said, realizing that if he'd been by himself, he would have been totally lost.

"Hey! Wait for me!" he called out as he began to run through the trees behind them.

# PART 40

Gloria stepped into the clearing and breathed a sigh of relief, as she saw the large bright-orange triangular object standing in front of the trees on the other side. She walked towards it followed by Sharn, then Julia and then Timothy. As soon as they neared it, the ship's door slid open and Klaus came to the open doorway.

"I was worried!" he said. "Are you all right? What happened?"

"Let's go inside," Gloria said. "It's not safe out here!"

Klaus stood aside to let her pass, then he saw Sharn, whom he stared at curiously. Sharn passed him, followed by Julia and Timothy. When they were all inside, Yuki touched a switch on the ship's control panel to close the door behind them. Timothy ran over to Jenny who was still lying completely bound, her eyes staring upward.

"How is she?" Timothy called back to Klaus.

"A typical zombie," Klaus said. "Agitated, growling and wild. Don't get too close to her!"

Timothy forced himself to remain a few feet away as he stared down at her. Jenny's eyes moved to the left to look up into his and she growled like a wild animal, pulling at the bonds with all her might trying to free herself.

"Do I know you?" Klaus said, walking over to Sharn to study his features.

Sharn looked at him, then an expression of recognition came onto his face.

"Klaus?" he said. "Erik's son?"

Klaus nodded, "I remember you! You came to the castle when I was younger. Your name is ... "

"Sharn," Sharn said.

Klaus nodded, "Sharn ... yes, I remember."

"It's good to see you again!" Sharn said. "You ... you were always so different from the others!" Sharn moved forward and hugged Klaus tightly.

"Then ... Klaus said, "we must be on the planet ... "

"Where it all began," Sharn said, finishing Klaus' sentence for him.

"So ... " Klaus began.

"We didn't go into the past," Gloria said, looking at him. "We went up!"

Sharn turned and saw Yuki staring at him curiously.

"You are ... a scientist," Yuki said.

"Sorry?" Sharn said, gazing at her strangely.

"The ship tells me that you are a scientist," Yuki said.

"The ... ship?" Sharn said, staring at Yuki.

"This is Yuki," Julia said. "She ... may seem a little weird. She seems to be able to communicate with the ship."

Sharn continued to stare at Yuki curiously.

"Interesting!" he said, obviously both amazed and intrigued.

Before anybody could say anything else, Timothy turned to them.

"Hey! Scientist man! Will you see to my girlfriend? Like, now!"

Sharn looked at him, then moved forward nodding, "Yes! Yes, of course!"

He took both the object which looked like a syringe and the vial with the green liquid from Timothy and knelt down beside Jenny. Klaus came over to help Timothy hold her still.

"Be careful she doesn't bite!" Gloria said, from behind them.

Timothy watched as Sharn put the liquid from the vial into the syringe-like object, then place it against Jenny's arm. Jenny growled up at him and snarled viciously as he pushed the liquid through the object and into her arm. When he was finished, Sharn stood up.

"Now we wait," he said.

Yuki moved over to stand beside Sharn. Sharn turned to look at her. Yuki was still staring at him strangely.

"Can ... can you really communicate with this ship?" Sharn asked.

"Yes," Yuki answered.

"What ... what does it say?"

Yuki put her head to one side, "She says, that you are a scientist."

"She?" said Julia, from behind.

Yuki looked at her, then nodded, "The ship's a girl," she said.

Julia stared at Yuki as if she were crazy, "Er ... yes, yes ... of course it is!"

Yuki turned back to Sharn, "She says that she was not completed, that she has some functions missing, that you, a scientist, can help her."

Sharn stared at her open-mouthed.

"Well, er ... I ... I can always have a look at it, er ... sorry! I ... I mean ... her!"

Yuki cocked her head to one side again as if she were listening, then she nodded, "She said that she would like that," Yuki said finally.

Julia looked at Gloria, "What do we do now?" she asked.

"That is obvious!" Sharn said, looking at them both. "We must go back to your planet, and we must kill Erik, we must kill them all!"

"And how do we do that?" Julia asked. "With these weapons?" She held up the laser gun that she was still holding.

Sharn grinned, "No, no! I ... I brought something."

Sharn took out  large round metallic ball from the bag he had been carrying on his shoulder.

"It's a bomb!" he said. "A special bomb.  I was going to use it to kill myself and all those creatures on this planet.  If we explode it within the prison dome, the blast will kill everything inside and the blast will be contained, it will not extend beyond the protective barrier."

"You mean, it's like ... some kind of nuclear bomb?" Gloria asked, staring down at the round metal object in Sharn's hand.

Sharn nodded, 'Exactly," he said.  "We must kill them all! Every single vampire and zombie!"

Both Gloria and Julia noticed Klaus staring at Sharn strangely.

Gloria turned to Yuki, "Can you get the ship to take us back?" she asked.

Yuki nodded, "Of course," she said.  "It's where she wants to go anyway."

# PART 41

The ship shook and vibrated as a deep machine-like whirring noise sounded.

"How do we know it's going back to the same place?" Julia asked, shouting above the noise of the machine and holding onto the control panel for support.

"Because it told me!" Yuki said, gazing up at the screen which was now blank.

"But what if ... ?" Julia began, and then stopped as both the noise and the vibrations ceased.

Julia breathed a sigh of relief.

"But what if we arrive somewhere else?" Julia said, finishing her sentence.

Yuki glanced at her, "We won't," she said.

Both Klaus and Gloria looked up at the screen, "We're back in the forest," Klaus said.

"Right back where we came from," Gloria agreed.

Yuki turned to Sharn, who was now studying the controls of the ship with interest, "She wants you to look at her," she said. "She says you will know how to fix her, how to make her complete."

"Fascinating!" Sharn said to himself. He stopped studying the controls and gazed up at the screen, "But ... no time!" he added. "Anyway, I'm not the genius that Erik was. I may not be able to fix anything!"

Yuki cocked her head to one side as if she were listening.

"She says she wants you to try," Yuki said.

"He says we have no time!" Gloria said, looking across at Yuki. She glanced at Sharn, "How do we do this?" she asked.

"All we have to do is set the bomb on a timer, then wait for it to explode."

"We have to get the innocent people out first!" Julia said. "There are the villagers, there are those still imprisoned in the castle!"

Gloria nodded, "She's right," she said to Sharn. "We can't detonate the bomb without freeing the innocent people first." Sharn looked at them both.

"It's risky," he said.

"But necessary," Julia added.

Sharn hesitated, then nodded, "Okay," he said, agreeing.

He placed the bomb onto the ship's control panel, "I'll show you how to use the timer and detonate the bomb," he said. "In case, er ... some of us don't come back, everyone has to know."

Julia glanced at Klaus who was standing with his head lowered.

"Are you okay?" she asked.

Klaus glanced up at her, then nodded.

"Are you sure?" Julia asked. "Sharn said we have to kill all of the vampires, but ... I'm sure he didn't mean you."

Klaus sighed. He watched Timothy stand up and walk over to them as Sharn began to explain how to set the bomb.

"It ... it's my family," Klaus said to Julia. "The only ... family I've ever known. He ... he's my father. I ... I know we have to stop this, but ... "

He glanced up and saw Gloria staring at him. She raised her laser gun, aiming it directly towards him.

"Gloria! No!" Julia shouted, quickly moving forward to stand between Klaus and Gloria.

"Sharn said 'all' of them," Gloria said, "and I have to agree. No more vampires! No more zombies! This has to end!"

"But ... he's helping us!" Julia protested.

"He was," Gloria said. "Not sure about now. You saw his eyes when Sharn spoke about killing them all. Erik's his father! Do you think he's just going to sit back and let us kill him?"

"Gloria ... please!" Julia pleaded.

'She ... she's right," Sharn said, looking at Gloria. "I ...I didn't mean Klaus. He ... he's different from the others. I saw that when he was just a child."

"He's a vampire!" Gloria said. "And we're about to kill his family! You can't tell me he's okay with that!"

Julia turned to look at Klaus.

"Klaus, how do you see your father?" she asked.

Klaus glanced down, "He ... he's a monster," he said.

Julia nodded, "Yes ... yes, he is. You understand what we must do, don't you?"

Klaus remained silent for a moment, then spoke, "I ... I thought the Time Machine ..." he said quietly, not looking up, "... you know ... if we go back in time ... we ... we could change what happened, what happened to him and to my uncle, if ... if we could only ... go back."

Sharn nodded sadly.

"There is no Time Machine," he said. "Only a Spaceship, a very ... " he glanced at Yuki, " ... interesting Spaceship!"

Sharn moved closer to Klaus, "And if this were a Time Machine, and we went back to change the past, what we would be doing is creating another dimension where things happen differently, but ... in this dimension, things will remain as they are."

Klaus stared at him, "So, in this world, nothing would change?"

Sharn shook his head, "Nothing would change," he said. "It would be like two roads going separately. If your father is not killed, he will stay on this road as a vampire, as a monster, but on the other road, the new dimension which we will have created, your father will have a chance to be himself again."

"I need to know," Gloria said, still aiming her laser gun at Klaus. "Will you try to stop us from killing your father?"

Julia turned from Gloria to look into Klaus' eyes. She saw the tears that were forming inside them.

Klaus shook his head, "No," he said, his voice almost a whisper.

"I wish that I could believe you!" Gloria said.

Julia turned once again to face her.

"Leave him alone!" she said. "If you kill him, you'll have to kill me too!"

Gloria studied her for a moment and saw the determination in Julia's eyes. She remained still, holding the laser gun towards them, then finally she lowered it.

Julia sighed with relief.

Gloria picked up the bag filled with weapons and threw it over her shoulder.

"Show us how to detonate the bomb," she said to Sharn.

Sharn showed them, and then, when he was finished, Gloria looked at Timothy.

"Are you coming?" she asked.

Timothy shook his head, "No, I ... I'll, stay, I'll stay here with Jenny," he said.

"I'll come," Yuki said.

Gloria looked at her and smiled, "No, you stay with the ship," she said.

She turned to look at both Sharn and Julia.

"It looks like it's just us three," she said.

"I'll come too," Klaus said.

Gloria hesitated, studying him with an expression of obvious distrust, then she nodded, "Okay, but you're with me!" she said. "And you'd better stay close!"

# PART 42

Gloria stared at Klaus' back as they walked through the trees towards the castle. Klaus stopped and turned to looked at her.

"I can feel you staring at me," he said. "If you want to kill me, why don't you just do it? Now! Right here!"

Gloria aimed her laser gun at him.

"I would!" she said. "If I thought you were leading me into a trap! The minute I feel there's something wrong, I 'will' kill you!"

Klaus raised his head and pointed to his neck.

"Here, I'll make it easy for you! ... Well? What are you waiting for?"

Gloria steadied her aim towards Klaus' neck.

"I don't need you!" she said. "Julia already told me where the prisoners are kept!"

"Not the hostages from the village," Klaus said. "Those prisoners are kept in a special place."

Gloria continued to stare at him, aiming her laser gun towards him, then finally, she lowered the gun.

"Show me where they are," She said. "But remember, I"ll be watching you all the way!"

In another part of the forest, Julia and Sharn were walking in the direction of the village where Julia had previously been drugged. Julia looked up at the full moon shining in the night sky and shivered. Even if she was carrying a weapon and was with someone, she still didn't feel safe walking in the forest, especially at night.

She glanced at Sharn who was walking beside her.

"So, how come you can speak English?" she asked.

Sharn looked at her with a grin

"I'm not," he said. "I"m speaking a language from my own planet. You understand it as English because of the translator waves."

Julia stopped walking, "Translator waves?" she asked. "What are they?"

"Something we developed a long time ago on my planet. All of our spaceships have them. It's a device which creates special electronic waves for the brain so that languages can be instantly translated into your own. Very practical if you travel to different planets and need to communicate with the natives."

"So ... you're saying that you are speaking another language, and I'm hearing it in English?" Julia said, astounded by the idea.

Sharn nodded,"And vice verse," he said. "It's standard Spaceship equipment."

They continued walking.

"Amazing!" Julia said to herself, shaking her head. "Do you know how long it took me to learn French?"

Sharn shrugged, "Two minutes?" he asked.

Julia looked at him and laughed, "Try five years!" she said. "And to think, I'm now speaking a language from another planet fluently!"

Sharn nodded, "Yes, you are."

Julia continued to shake her head in amazement.

"You'll have to show me this translation thing," she said. "On this planet, I'll be a millionaire! ... No ... a billionaire!"

Suddenly, there was a loud growling sound and four zombies appeared from between the trees moving towards them. Both Julia and Sharn fired their laser guns at the same time aiming for the zombies' necks. to decapitate them. Within seconds, the four zombies fell headless to the ground.

"Nice shooting!" Sharn said to Julia with a grin.

Julia shrugged, "I think I'm getting used to this," she said.

She glanced down at the zombie bodies, "Let's go. I think the village is this way," Julia said, pointing straight ahead.

Sharn gestured with his hand, "After you," he said.

"Ah! A gentleman from another planet yet!" Julia said, gazing at him with a smile.

"We try our best," Sharn said with a smile, following after her.

Both Gloria and Klaus looked up at the castle from behind some bushes.

"So," Gloria said. "Where do you keep the prisoners?"

"There are two places," Klaus said. "The prisoners for food or turning are kept in the basement. That's where you found Julia and Yuki. The other prisoners are from the village, they are unharmed. My father lets the villagers see their family members and friends from time to time, it assures their obedience. They are held in the tower."

Klaus pointed to one of the towers rising up from the castle.

"Guards?" Gloria asked, looking up at the tall tower.

"The chamber is always locked," Klaus said, "so only one guard is outside the chamber's door. Another comes regularly to bring the food."

"So, how do we get up there?" Gloria asked.

"There are only two ways," Klaus said. "Enter the castle and take the stairs, or climb up the outside wall."

Gloria studied the tower for a moment.

"I think I prefer the stairs," she said.

Klaus looked at her, "I could climb up the outside wall," he said. "But I know you don't trust me."

"We'll take the stairs," Gloria said, meeting his gaze. "I want you where I can see you."

Klaus seemed to smile briefly, then he nodded and looked back up at the castle, "Okay," he said.

Gloria climbed the outside wall of the castle towards the open window she had entered earlier which had been the window to Timothy's bedroom. She reached the window and climbed inside, then turned to help Klaus, who was climbing up the wall behind her, but Klaus had been climbing the wall easily and required absolutely no help from her. He climbed into the room behind her, and then they both went across to the door. Gloria opened it slightly and they both remained still, listening. There was no noise. Gloria opened the door wider and looked out into the corridor. It was empty. The whole castle was silent and seemed completely deserted.

"Which way?" Gloria asked.

"Left," Klaus said. "We go along the corridor, down the stairs into a small courtyard, and then cross the courtyard to the tower."

"Okay," Gloria said, gripping the laser gun tightly in her hands, "let's go!"

They moved out of the room and along the corridor, walking slowly, the floorboards creaking beneath their feet, disturbing the silence as they advanced.

Suddenly, the floorboards creaked behind them and they both turned to see Annoncietta standing at the other end of the corridor staring at them with her hands on her hips. Annoncietta grinned wickedly, her eyes turning bright red.

"Hello Klaus!" she hissed.

"Go!" Klaus said to Gloria, who was standing beside him. "I'll handle this!"

Gloria looked at him, then at Annoncietta.

Klaus dropped his laser gun to the floor, then Gloria saw his special knife appear from down his sleeve and into his hand.

"Klaus!" Gloria said.

"I said go!" Klaus said, looking at her.

Gloria stared back at him, then moved backwards, turned, and started to run further along the corridor leaving Klaus behind her.

Annoncietta's grin widened as she stared at Klaus and she hissed once again.

"Kissy kissy, little Klaussy!" Annoncietta hissed.

And then her expression changed to a horrible sneer, and she leapt forward and flew along the corridor towards Klaus, hissing and showing her fangs, her clawed fingers reaching forward in front of her as she flew towards him.

Gloria reached the staircase at the end of the corridor and heard growling, hissing and screaming sounds coming from behind her as she ran down the stairs as fast as she could. She reached the bottom, looked out across the small courtyard, and then ran towards the tower on the opposite side. Two vampires suddenly appeared from the left, their eyes bright red as they growled, baring their fangs, and ran towards her. Gloria stopped and spun round to face them, raising her laser gun in their direction. She fired, hitting one vampire in the neck, severing his head from his body. The vampire's body fell to the ground and exploded in a cloud of dust as the other vampire, a young woman, leapt forward, seeming to fly towards her. She hit Gloria knocking her back onto the ground before Gloria could fire another laser blast. The vampire was now on top of her, growling and hissing wildly as Gloria wrestled with her, trying to avoid the vampire's claws and fangs as they approached her neck. Gloria kneed the vampire in the side, knocking the vampire off her and managed to get up onto her knees. She pulled a silver knife from her belt and stabbed the vampire in the heart just as the vampire was about to attack her again. The vampire screamed, its skin cracking, and then it exploded in a cloud of dust. She watched as the dust slowly began to drift away on the night's gentle breeze. Gloria breathed a sigh of relief, then put the knife back into her belt, grabbed the laser gun where it had fallen and stood up.  She paused, looking towards the tower in front of her, then ran towards it and entered.

# PART 43

The village was in darkness and once again seemed deserted as both Julia and Sharn walked through the village streets. As they rounded a corner, they saw lights coming from only one building, the Inn. They walked towards it, holding their weapons ready to fire and looking around carefully at the surrounding darkened streets as they went. When they reached the Inn's door, Julia glanced at Sharn's strange looking clothing.

"They might be surprised at you," she said. "Let me do the talking."

Sharn nodded, "As you wish," he said.

Julia turned back to the Inn's door, then pushed it open and went inside followed by Sharn. Once again, the Inn's customers, who were sitting around at various tables and at the bar, stopped talking and turned to look at them as they came in. Julia raised the laser gun in her hands so that they could see it clearly and stared back at each of them. A curtain moved aside from the other end of the bar and Rose appeared. She stopped in her tracks, her eyes widening as she recognized Julia and saw the laser gun in her hands. The barman, who had been cleaning glasses at the other end of the bar, lowered his hands beneath the counter. Julia turned, aiming her laser gun towards him.

"Keep your hands where I can see them!" she said, in a commanding tone.

The barman froze, staring at the laser gun aimed towards him. Julia gazed at the customers and at Rose, all of whom were staring towards her in silence.

"We mean you no harm," Julia said. "We know the vampires have members of your families and and friends in the castle and force you to work for them."

"What is it you want then?" Rose asked, continuing to stare at the laser gun in Julia's hands.

"We want to help you," Julia said.

Gloria went up the twisting staircase of the tower as fast as she could. She was near the top when she heard someone talking. Gloria stopped and listened. She gripped the laser gun tightly in her hands and continued to move on up the staircase slowly. When the last few steps were in front of her, she paused. She advanced slowly, then leaned forward and peeped around the wall and into the corridor on her left, in the direction the voices were coming from.

She saw two guards, two male vampires. One of them was sitting on a chair next to a large wooden door, while another was standing in front of him talking. Gloria remained still for a moment, then took a deep breath and stepped out into the corridor leveling her laser gun towards them. The first blast knocked the one who was standing back onto the floor. The other vampire jumped quickly up from its chair growling and baring its fangs towards her. Gloria fired, but the second vampire was fast, it leapt to the side and onto the wall, and then, just as if it were a spider, it moved quickly along the side of the wall towards her. Gloria fired again, and then again, each time missing the vampire as it moved too fast, avoiding the laser blasts, and then it was above her. It leapt down from the side of the wall and onto her, knocking her to the floor. Gloria raised the laser gun again, firing, hitting the vampire's arm, and the vampire growled loudly and  angrily, its fangs moving towards her neck.

Gloria cried out, trying to push the vampire away with all her might, but the vampire was too strong her. Its fangs moved closer, closer, closer towards Gloria's neck. Gloria cried out once more, and then suddenly, the vampire screamed and arched backwards up away from her. Gloria watched in amazement as the vampire's skin began to crack, and then it exploded into dust just above her. She looked up, wondering what had happened, and then saw Klaus standing over her with his special knife in his hand. There was another growl as the other vampire Gloria had hit with a blast from her laser gun got up and now started to run towards them. Klaus quickly raised his arm and threw his knife towards it. The knife hit the vampire in the heart. The vampire screamed as its skin began to crack, and then, within seconds, all that was left of the vampire was a cloud of dust. Klaus looked down at Gloria and offered her his hand to help her up. Gloria stared up at him, then took his hand and pulled herself up onto her feet.

"Thanks," she said.

Klaus nodded, avoiding eye contact, then turned and went over to pick up his knife.

"Nice knife," Gloria said, glancing down the special silver knife in Klaus' hand.

"It was a present from my mother," Klaus said. "Just in case."

Gloria watched as Klaus walked over to the large wooden door the vampire had been guarding. Klaus placed his hand over the lock and then she heard a click.

"You don't need a key?" Gloria asked.

Klaus looked at her, "Vampires never need keys," he said.

He placed his hand on the handle and opened the door. The dimly chamber inside was like a large prison cell. There were no seats, no beds, only straw on the floor. At least twenty people looked up at them when they entered. Some of them were women and children. There were a few young men, but most of the men looked old with beards. Their clothes were ragged, and their skin was white, as if they were undernourished. As Gloria stared down at them in a mixture of both shock and horror, tears came into her eyes. Each of the prisoners stared up at them in fear and cowered away from them.

"Don't worry," Gloria said softly, with emotion in her voice. "We've come to free you."

# PART 44

"Is everyone here?" Julia asked, looking at Rose, as the villagers began to follow both Julia and Sharn along the dark deserted village streets.

"This is everyone," Rose replied. "There were originally over two hundred people in the village before the vampires came. The vampires killed many of them, took them for food. Families and friends of those left alive were taken to the castle as hostages to force the surviving villagers to work for them. That began a few centuries ago, but over time, new generations were born, both in the village and in captivity in the castle, and sometimes, they take new hostages from the village, and so ... it continues. As you can see, there are not many of us."

"What about the zombies?" Sharn asked, looking at her.

'The village and this part of the forest is forbidden to them," Rose said. "It"s part of the truce."

Rose looked at Julia, "Your friends ... what if they get caught? What if they can't help our families and friends to escape?"

Julia stopped walking and turned to her, "You must have faith," she said.

"I promise, they'll do everything they can. This nightmare ... your nightmare ... it has to stop."

Rose stared at her, then glanced down and nodded, "You are right," she said. "You are right, it has to stop."

Julia looked at the villagers following behind and felt a sadness for them. She turned and continued walking, gripping her laser gun tightly in her hands and with a grim determination on her face to lead these people out of their slavery, out of their darkness, and into the light.

Gloria led the freed prisoners across the castle's courtyard towards the main entrance. She glanced round and saw Klaus bringing up the rear and gazing carefully around behind them as they went. The reached the huge main doors leading out of the castle and Klaus ran up past the freed prisoners to join Gloria.

"I can open the doors,"Klaus said.

Gloria watched as he moved to the right of the doors and touched something hidden on the wall beside them. Within seconds, both doors started to creak slowly open.

"You take them out," Klaus said to Gloria. "I'll go down to the base-ment and free any other prisoners down there."

Gloria glanced round at the castle behind her. It stood rising up to the moonlit sky like a dark and brooding monster. She listened to the silence as the night breeze blew her blonde hair into her eyes. She brushed her hair aside.

"It's almost too easy," she said. "Something's wrong."

Klaus looked back up at the castle, "Maybe not," he said. "Maybe for once, easy is good." He looked back at Gloria, "Take them to safety, I"ll get the others."

Gloria stared at him for a moment, then nodded, gripping the laser gun tightly, unable to shake the chilling feeling that she was going to need it again. As the freed prisoners started leaving the castle through the open main doors, Klaus turned to run back to free the prisoners left in the basement.

"Klaus!" Gloria called out, watching him go.

Klaus stopped to look back at her.

"Be careful," Gloria said, gazing at him, her eyes now showing concern.

Klaus smiled, then turned and ran back towards the castle.

# PART 45

Erik Stolz stared out at the departing freed prisoners from his study window. Sinella, who was standing beside him, rested her head on his shoulder.

"I could go out there and kill them all if you wish it," Sinella said.

Erik turned to her, "I'm sure you could my dear. But ... I have been thinking. Why worry about the prisoners? As you know, I have been planning something for our future. Soon, we will be gone from this place. I have sent our vampire slaves to wipe out everyone in the village, their usefulness is fulfilled. You may go up to the battlements and howl to them. Tell them that other meat is on the way and that tonight, they may feast as much as they wish."

Sinella leaned forward and kissed Erik lightly on the cheek.

"And what of your son?" she asked. "What of Klaus?"

Erik turned to stare at her, his eyes turning red as if an anger seemed to fire up inside him, and then his anger left him and he grinned, "I will deal with my son," he said.

Sinella smiled at him, then gave Erik one more kiss before gliding across the floor of the study to the door, her feet not touching the ground. Erik watched her leave, then glanced towards the flames of the fire that was burning brightly in the fireplace, thinking of Klaus, thinking of his only son. A sneer suddenly etched its way across his face as he whispered one word to himself.

"Klaus!" he whispered, his eyes now burning brightly with anger once again.

"How far is this boundary?" Sharn asked, glancing at Rose, who was walking beside him along the road that led out of the village and through the forest.

"Not far now," Rose said. "Like I said, zombies don't come to this part of the forest, we're safe from them as long as we stay on this road leading out. It's vampires we have to worry about."

"They have your family?" Sharn asked.

"My brother," Rose said. "He's the only family I have now. You're plan had better work, or our families ... "

Rose stopped talking and glanced down sadly as she walked, " ... our families will die," she said.

Sharn stared at her, then put a reassuring hand on her arm, "Don't worry. We'll get you and your brother out of this."

They walked in silence for a moment, side by side. Rose looked at Julia who was walking further along the road in front of them, "What is she? Your daughter or something?" she asked.

Sharn chuckled, "No, she's just a friend. She's a very ... very brave young girl."

Rose nodded, "Yes, she is."

She continued gazing after Julia, and then sighed, "Did she tell you? I ... I almost handed her over to the vampires."

"She told me," Sharn said. "But you were a victim, like all these other people from the village."

Sharn gestured back to the villagers who were following along the road behind them.

Rose glanced down sadly, "She's right," she said. "One way or another, this has to stop."

Suddenly, Julia stopped walking in front of them and gestured back to the others to do the same.

"What is it?" Rose asked, staring at Julia who now seemed to be listening.

"I think she's heard something," Sharn said, "she has very good ears."

He glanced round, but saw only the villagers standing still on the road behind them. The next instant, there was a scream.

Then they heard a howl, then many howls accompanied by loud growling sounds. The vampires appeared from out of the trees behind them. Julia cried out and ran back to where Sharn and Rose were standing. Both Julia and Sharn moved to the side of the road to aim their laser guns back at the now approaching vampires.

Rose looked at the other villagers and cried out one word, "Stakes!" she shouted.

Each of the villagers, now facing the vampires, brought out pointed wooden stakes from their clothing.

Rose glanced at Sharn, who seemed surprised, "We never go anywhere without them!" she said.

"I hope everybody's ready to fight!" Julia said, gripping her laser gun tightly as the vampires approached them along the road.

"Believe me, we're ready!" Rose said, staring at the vampires with a strong determined look as they came closer, growling and baring their fangs as if they were wild animals.

Gloria led the ragged group of freed prisoners through the woods. They exited into a small clearing and Gloria paused.

"Keep closer!" she said, glancing back to them. "Don't fall back, we have to stay together!"

Suddenly, one of the freed prisoners, a young man, stopped and pointed towards something he had seen. Gloria looked round and saw the zombies. There were about thirty of them. They were all standing in a line on the other side of the clearing as if they had been waiting for them. The zombies growled, clawing at the air in front of them as if they were impatient to attack and devour them. Gloria saw Klaus' uncle standing among them, his eyes glowing bright green as he stared across the clearing beneath the silvery light of the moon above. Green Eyes seemed to grin, then he let out a cry and each of the zombies started to move forward across the clearing towards them, growling loudly like wild beasts.

"Run!" Gloria shouted, turning to the people behind her. "Quick! Follow me!"

The freed prisoners didn't need to be told twice. They ran, following Gloria across the small clearing to the right and into the trees, running as fast as they could. Two of the older men fell and tried weakly to pick themselves up, but the zombies were moving faster than they thought and were quickly upon them. Gloria stopped, glancing back, as the screams from the two elderly freed prisoners pierced the night air. She saw the zombies on the men's bodies, biting and clawing at them wildly as the two elderly men screamed horribly from the terrible pain.

"Go! Go! Go!" Gloria shouted, as she turned to the group of freed prisoners who were now running through the trees and bushes. Gloria aimed her laser gun back at the approaching zombies and fired. The blast hit one of the leading zombies in the chest, went right through it, and hit the zombies who were following closely behind. The zombies fell, but instead of staying down, tried to get back up onto their feet. Gloria fired another blast decapitating a zombie who had moved around them, its headless body falling and its head now rolling along the ground towards her. Gloria took out a small disc grenade, took off the safety and pressed the button, just as Sharn had showed her, and then she threw it. Quickly, she turned and ran, following the freed prisoners through the bushes and trees, hearing the sound of the explosion and the cries from the zombies behind her as she went.

# PART 46

Sinella stood on the high battlements of the castle gazing down at the scenery below. She saw the yellow, red and orange flames from the explosion in the woods rising up into the night. A sneer pulled at Sinella's lips as she stared at the explosion. Suddenly, she put her head back, and, gazing up at the full moon, gave a loud eerie sounding howl.

Klaus looked up, hearing the howl from where he was at the top of a staircase leading down towards the basement. As he reached the basement floor, he listened, taking out his special knife and held it ready. He heard no sound. Turning the corner, he moved to the left across the dimly-lit basement hall towards the passage on the other side. Suddenly, he heard a noise to his right and spun round. A young male vampire flew across the hall to hit him and knocked him to the floor. The vampire was now on top of him clawing towards his neck and growling with his fangs bared. Klaus managed to grab the vampire's claw-like hands and force him onto his side. They rolled on the floor, both of them growling, and then Klaus was on top of the other vampire. They struggled for a moment, then Klaus saw his knife where it had fallen. He reached out for it, but as he did so the other vampire was able to hit him and push him off. Klaus rolled to the side, grasping his knife as he did so, and then the other vampire fell on top of him, but Klaus was ready. Quickly, with his knife now gripped firmly in his hand, he thrust the silver blade up into the vampire's heart. The vampire cried out, arched back away from Klaus, grasping at the wound in its heart, and then exploded into a cloud of dust. Klaus lay for a moment, sighing, then he got up onto his feet, and once again headed towards the passage across the hall. He entered the passage and halfway along it, he stopped and put his hand against the wall to his right. The wall suddenly started to move, sliding to the left and opening up to show another narrow passage which lay in front of him. Along the dimly-lit passage, there were cells on either side. As he walked along the passage, he saw human figures crouching in the cells behind the bars. Their eyes glowed red and they growled as he passed.

Further along the passage, he came to a large cell on his right and looked inside. Three young men and five young girls were huddled together and shaking in fear, holding onto one another for comfort. Klaus placed his hand against the lock and the cell door clicked open. The prisoners moved back away from him as he entered, staring up at him with wide frightened eyes. Three of the girls began to whimper.

"Come," Klaus said. "I'm here to free you."

'But ... but you're one of them!" said one of the girls, pointing up to him, her hand visibly shaking as she spoke. "You ... You're a vampire!"

"It must be a trick!" one of the young men said, staring up at Klaus. "Don't trust him!"

Klaus gazed down at them as they cowered away from him.

"Either you come with me, or you stay here," he said. "It's your choice."

He remained a moment longer, gazing down at them, then he turned and left the cell.

"Do you trust him?" one of the girls said to a young man beside her.

The young man stared at the open cell door, then stood up, "I ...I don't know," he said. "But ... but I'm not going to stay here!"

He moved towards the cell door.

"He's right," said another young man standing up, "I don't trust him, but ... we have no choice!"

The second young man also moved towards the cell door. The remaining prisoners sat looking at each other, then they too stood up. Each of them hesitated as they reached the open cell door, looking out into the narrow passage before stepping out of the cell. One by one, the prisoners came along the passage towards Klaus who was standing at the passage entrance waiting for them.

Klaus regarded them for a moment as they reached him, then smiled, "This way," he said, turning.

# PART 47

As Klaus emerged from the passage back into the basement hall, he saw his father standing there, waiting for him. Klaus stopped in his tracks, gazing across at him.

"Father," he said.

The prisoners Klaus had freed stepped out of the passage behind him and stopped. They stared fearfully at Erik Stolz who was standing with his hands clasped tightly together on the other side of the hall watching them.

"My son," Erik said, now staring fixedly into Klaus' eyes.

"Father ... " Klaus said, " ... we ... we can't go on like this! This ... killing!"

Erik Stolz smiled as he stared at his son, "You were always weak," he said.

"I should never have listened to your mother. If you'd drunk human blood, you'd have been stronger, but it's too late for that now, isn't it?"

Klaus stared back at him in silence for a moment.

"You lied to me," he said, finally. "You said you were building a Time Machine, you said you wanted to go back, change the past, but instead, all you wanted to do was go back to Genera, the planet where it all started, and destroy the antidote that our people were creating."

"That antidote would have killed us all!" Erik shouted angrily. "You don't see? How strong we are? We're so much stronger than these humans! We're stronger than any other species! We live on Klaus! We're immortal, like Gods! If we spread across planets, across the universe, we will be worshiped! We will have slaves at our feet! I could not let our people create an antidote that would stop us. So, yes! I lied and created a ship, a Spaceship, but much more sophisticated than any normal Spaceship! My ship can travel to places, to other worlds, in an instant! Klaus, I want you to reign by my side. Together we will be supreme rulers! Far greater than any ruler who ever lived!"

Erik raised his arm and put out his hand towards his son.

"Come Klaus! Let us rule whole universes ... together!"

Klaus remained still, staring at his father in silence.

"No," he said, finally.

Erik looked at the freed prisoners who were standing behind Klaus. They were staring across at him, their eyes wide with fear as their bodies visibly shook uncontrollably.

"You will give all that up, for them?" Erik said, staring at the frightened group of people standing behind Klaus. "Look at them!" Erik shouted. "They are weak! Unworthy even to beg at our feet!"

"They are human!" Klaus said. "As mother once was! As ... Amy once was."

Erik studied his son's face, then smiled, "Ah, yes ... Amy! The girl you fell in love with."

"You didn't have to make her a vampire!" Klaus shouted.

"I did it for you," Erik said. "For you ... my son."

Klaus shook his head, "I have seen you change," he said. "I've seen you become different! You no longer have any feelings inside you! You have become ... a monster father!"

"Then ... my son," Erik said, gripping his hands tightly together, "... there is nothing more to be said, is there?"

Erik let out a loud cry! The cry was deafening! His face was now distorted into a mask of anger, his eyes blazing red,

and then suddenly, he leapt forward and began flying towards his son with a banshee-like scream filling the basement hall and making the freed prisoners tremble even more, in pure uncontrolled fear.

# PART 48

Julia fired a laser blast and decapitated a vampire, its head falling onto the rain-drenched road. The vampires attacked and the villagers fought back trying to plunge their stakes into vampire hearts. Several of the villagers cried out as the vampires knocked them to the ground and sank their fangs into their necks. Rose struck a vampire in the chest with her stake and watched it explode in a cloud of dust as Sharn fought beside her blasting a vampire to the ground with his laser gun only to see the vampire stand up once again and charge towards him in anger.

Sharn cursed himself for not firing at the vampire's neck, and this time he aimed carefully, decapitating it. The vampire's head flew off from the blast hitting another vampire behind it as its body fell headless to the ground and then exploded, the dust rising up from it. Sharn turned just in time to see a vampire about to leap onto Julia from behind and fired quickly, not having enough time to aim for its neck. The vampire cried out and fell back onto the ground. Julia turned, saw what had happened and fired down at it, the blast cutting off the vampire's head from its body before it had time to get back up. As she turned back to Sharn, she saw him staring at her with wide eyes, and then he fell to his knees. She saw the vampire standing behind him growling viciously as it retrieved its bloody claws from inside Sharn's body.

"Sharn!" Julia cried out.

She ran forward and smashed the vampire in the face with the butt of the laser gun. The vampire fell back, then she aimed her gun down at it and fired, blasting its neck away from its body. The vampire exploded, and quickly, Julia knelt down beside Sharn. Sharn looked up at her, his eyes half closed, then weakly, he reached up his hand to touch her face. He tried to speak, then his face froze, and his eyes remained open, staring up, unseeing. Julia lowered her head sadly as tears formed in her eyes.

"Sharn ... " she said, softly.

Gloria ran through the woods hearing the loud growling sounds of the zombies coming from somewhere behind her. Occasionally she glanced back as she ran but saw nothing through the surrounding trees and bushed. One of the freed prisoners began lagging behind, an elderly man, and she ran over to him, grabbing his arm.

"Thomas!" she heard a woman cry, as the woman, who was younger, came running back to help him. The woman grabbed Thomas' other arm.

"Keep moving!" Gloria shouted, letting go of Thomas' arm and watching them leave, then she raised her laser gun to turn and face the approaching zombies. She glanced back once more at the woman helping Thomas away, "Go! Go!" she shouted after them, then first zombie appeared, emerging through the bushes and moving towards her. Gloria fired, hitting its neck and decapitating it, and then another appeared running jerkily, almost stumbling over the body of the first zombie which had fallen. Gloria fired again blasting the zombie's head away from its body. Three more zombies moved through the bushes and others appeared from behind the trees coming towards her. Gloria fired one more laser blast missing a zombie's neck and hitting another zombie behind in the chest. Gloria turned and ran as more zombies appeared growling angrily and running jerkily after her.

Julia watched as the few remaining vampires retreated back along the road leaving behind them the dead bodies of the villagers they had killed. The small group of village survivors remained still, staring at the retreating vampires, holding their sharply pointed wooden stakes tightly in their hands. Julia walked among the dead bodies stepping over them and staring down at them. Suddenly, she stopped and gazed down at one body she recognized. Rose lay on the ground, a pool of blood around her. Julia remained still for a moment, then knelt down beside her. Rose's eyes opened and Julia gasped, surprised to find that she was still alive after losing so much blood.

Rose stared up at her, then moved her mouth, trying to speak.

"My ... my brother!" she managed to whisper. "S ... save my ... my brother!"

Rose let out a long sigh, and then she stopped breathing, her eyes, now unseeing, continuing to stare up at Julia.

Julia lowered her head sadly. After a moment, she heard other survivors from the villagers also walking among the dead bodies and crying as they knelt down beside family members and friends. Julia glanced up and watched them for a moment, then she saw Sharn's dead body lying on the road not far away and she stared at it. Tears rolled down her face as she remained still, staring.

Suddenly, one of the dead bodies seemed to gasp and sit up. It growled, its eyes turning red as it bared its fangs towards a nearby villager, a woman. One of the other villagers ran over to it, and, with a cry of rage, plunged his pointed stake into the creature's heart. The new vampire screamed, its hands clawing towards the villager, and then it exploded, its dust slowly dispersing on the night's gentle breeze. Julia stood up looking at the remaining villagers, "We should go," she said. "They'll be back."

The villagers nodded, glancing down sadly at the surrounding bodies strewn across the road. A few of them remained still, sobbing, then they began to follow Julia as she turned and walked once more along the wet rain-swept road, gripping the laser gun tightly in her hands as she went.

# PART 49

Klaus fell to the floor grunting and rolling as his father stared down at him and approached him once more. Erik leaned down and picked his son up with only one hand grasped around Klaus' throat, and with, what seemed like superhuman strength, he threw Klaus across the hall. Once more, Klaus grunted as he hit the floor. He rolled to the side, trying to stand up. The freed prisoners stared at the scene in front of them in horror, cowering back against the wall near the entrance to the passage.

"You are weak!" Erik shouted down to his son, walking slowly over to him. "Sensitive! Like your mother!"

He reached Klaus and picked him up again with one hand gripping his throat. Klaus hung from his father's grasp with feet off the floor as Erik now began to squeeze his son's throat strongly.

"It is a pity," Erik said, staring into Klaus' eyes as Klaus hung gasping from his father's grip. "We could have reigned together! Father and son!"

Erik's eyes burned bright red as he spoke.

"Instead, you must die!"

Klaus' choking gasps grew louder as Erik now squeezed his son's throat even stronger.

"No!" came a sudden cry from across the hall.

Erik turned to see the little hunchbacked servant running towards him.

"Master! No!" the hunchbacked cried.

Erik turned to stare at him, his bright red eyes blazing wildly.

"Candor?" Erik cried out loudly. "You dare tell me what to do?"

"Master! He ... he's your son!" the hunchback said, gazing up at Erik.

Erik looked back at Klaus, whose body was now beginning to grow limp beneath his grip. Candor, the hunchback, glanced around with panicked eyes searching for something, anything, that he could use to stop Erik from killing Klaus. He saw Klaus' special knife where it had fallen to the floor and ran across to pick it up. He held it in his hand, staring down at it, then he grasped the handle tightly and looked back up at Erik, who, with one hand, seemed to be squeezing the life away from Klaus.

"Pain!" Erik said, gazing into Klaus' eyes. "First, the pain! Feel your life slowly ebb away! Then, I will cut off your head!"

"I ... I'm sorry master," Candor said softly, as he watched Erik, then, with an ears-splitting yell, he ran towards Erik and jumped up onto his back. Erik cried out, dropping Klaus who fell to the floor choking and gasping and clutching at his throat. The hunchback remained on Erik's back, his arm around Erik's throat holding on tightly as Erik tried to throw him off. The hunchback raised Klaus' special knife. It seemed to gleam in the dim light from the burning torches hanging from the basement hall's walls, then the hunchback plunged it down into Erik's chest, again and again, and again, until, at last, he struck Erik's heart. Erik screamed, arched back, and finally managed to knock Candor off his back, but it was too late. Candor fell to the floor and rolled, then looked up and saw Erik stumble forward a few steps, screaming wildly, and then his body exploded with a loud bang, and a huge cloud of dust burst out across the hall almost covering it entirely.

Candor remained on the floor for a moment staring up at the cloud of dust, then he got to his feet and quickly ran over to Klaus who lay on the floor, his hands gripping at his throat and gasping for breath.

"Klaus! Klaus!" The hunchback cried, kneeling down beside him. "My son! Are you all right? I ... I could never let him hurt you! I ... I raised you, looked after you, as if you were my own son!"

Klaus looked up at him, as he gasped trying to catch his breath, a dim red light glowing in his eyes.

"Help ... help them!" Klaus managed to say, pointing a finger towards the freed prisoners who were staring across at them with wide fear-filled eyes and still cowering against the wall near the passage.

"Help me ... to ... to save them!" Klaus managed to say.

Candor glanced across at the cowering freed prisoners, then back down at Klaus.

"I will!" Candor said, down to him.

"I promise, I will!"

# PART 50

Gloria ran through the woods following behind the freed prisoners and came to another clearing. They ran across it as quickly as they could hearing the wild growling of the zombies coming from behind. As they reached the other side and were once again about to enter the trees, Gloria glanced back and noticed something strange. The zombies, who had been chasing them, suddenly stopped. They stood in a long line across the clearing behind them growling and clawing at the air towards them angrily, and yet, for some reason, not daring to move forward across the clearing as if there were an invisible barrier which stopped them. Gloria stood looking back at them curiously, wondering why they had stopped. Green Eyes, Klaus' uncle, stepped forward between the line of zombies and stood staring across at her angrily, his green eyes burning brightly as if they had a light inside them. He growled loudly, an angry sneer appearing on his face as he stared across the clearing at her. Gloria turned and ran into the trees following behind the freed prisoners who were running through the forest in front of her.

"The road!" she heard one of them cry out. "The road!"

The other freed prisoners cried out in delight as they stepped out from the trees and onto the road. Gloria followed them onto the road and stood looking at them with a curious expression on her face.

"The road!" one young man said, turning to her. "The zombies! They can't come to the road! It's the truce! The truce they have with the vampires!"

The older ones knelt down on the road to rest and get their breaths back. Suddenly, the freed prisoners who were laughing and rejoicing stopped as they stared along the road to the far end. Gloria followed their gaze and saw what they were looking at. Farther along the road, and coming towards them, was what seemed at first to be a small group of people. But as they came closer, they saw that they were not really people.

"Vampires!" Gloria shouted, staring towards them.

Sinella went down the steps and into the basement. The dimly-lit basement hall was empty. In the silence, Sinella felt something and stopped still. She gazed around the hall, listening, then moved forward slowly, looking around the hall as she went. Suddenly she stopped, gazing down at the dust which covered the floor. She stared at it, then knelt down, touched the dust softly, then picked up a handful of it and let it run through her fingers.

"Erik," she said, softly.

A sadness came over her. She lowered her head, remaining silent for a few moments, then suddenly, she threw her head back and screamed, then howled, her eyes burning bright red as she growled upwards, grasping tightly at what remained of the dust in her hand.

Klaus, now weak, staggered through the woods with Candor at his side and the freed prisoners following behind.

"Are you all right?" Candor asked, looking up at him with concern in his eyes.

Klaus nodded as he staggered on.

"We ... we have to ... get them to safety," he managed to say.

"I know," Candor said. "It is your wish, and I will always stand by you."

Klaus stopped to look down at him.

"You ... you have always been ... like a father to me Candor," he said. "More so than ... my real father."

Candor smiled," I brought you up, took care of you ever since you were a baby. I could let no harm come to you."

Klaus dropped down to his knees, then placed his arms tightly around Candor.

"Thank you!" Klaus said, as he hugged the hunchback with tears in his eyes. "Thank you!"

The freed prisoners stood staring down at them in amazement.

"Candor, "Klaus said, now pulling away to look into Candor's eyes. "Can you ... can you take them to the road? Lead them out, past ... past the barrier? You must go to."

Candor nodded, "Of course!" he said.  "But ... what of you?"

Klaus lowered his head, "I ... I must do something," he said.

Candor stared up at him sadly, then leaned forward and hugged Klaus tightly.  Klaus hugged him back, then pulled away, and with some difficulty, stood up.

"Goodbye Candor," he said, gazing down at the hunchback.

Klaus looked up and glanced at the freed prisoners, then he turned and walked to the left, staggering a little, through the trees and out of sight.

"Goodbye ... my son," Candor said, staring sadly after him.

# PART 51

Gloria stood ready, standing in the road in front of the freed prisoners as the small band of vampires approached them. She raised the laser gun, aiming it at the vampire who was walking in front of the others and prepared to fire.

"Keep behind me," she said to the freed prisoners, who were standing behind her and holding each other with frightened expressions.

Suddenly, they heard a loud howling sound. It filled the night air. It was long, eerie-sounding and, strangely, seemed sad, as if it were a wild beast in lament, weeping somewhere, and howling up at the moon. The vampires stopped moving towards them. They raised their heads, listening to the long lament of the howling that seemed to pierce the night's darkness as if it were a thousand tears transformed into sound.

Gloria watched the vampires curiously as they remained still, listening, and gazing up at the moon. The vampire in front threw its head back and began to howl, then the others did the same, and then, they stopped. The leading vampire lowered its head and stared towards Gloria with hate-filled burning red eyes, then quickly it turned and ran off the road followed by the others and disappeared through the trees of the forest on their left.

"What ... just happened?" one of the freed prisoners said behind Gloria.

Gloria remained staring at trees through which the vampires had disappeared, then slowly she lowered her laser gun.

"I don't know," she said softly, wondering the same thing to herself.

She turned, looking at the people behind her, then nodded towards the road in front of them, "Come on! Let's go! Before they change their minds and come back!"

Sinella stood high up on the battlements of the castle, howling tearfully up at the full moon in the night sky above her. In her hand, she still had the dust she had picked up off the basement floor. she howled again and again and kept howling as tears ran down her cheeks, a figure dressed all in white, like a ghost, in the darkness of the night.

Jenny opened her eyes and stared up into Timothy's face. Timothy smiled down at her and caressed her cheek gently.

"How are you feeling?" he asked softly.

Jenny remained silent, not moving, then suddenly she leaned up onto her elbows and glanced round.

"Wh ... where are we?" she asked. "What happened?"

She saw Yuki who was standing near the ship's control panel and staring across at her strangely.

"We're safe," Timothy said.

"Safe?" Jenny repeated, turning to look into his eyes.

"Safe from what? What happened?"

She looked around, "Where are we?"

Then she pointed towards Yuki, "And ... Who ... who's this?

"That's Yuki," Timothy said. "She's a friend." He turned to Yuki, "Say hello to my girlfriend, Jenny," he said.

"Hello Jenny," Yuki said, her expression remaining emotionless as she continued to stare across at her.

"You ... don't remember anything?" Timothy asked, gazing back down at Jenny.

Jenny stared up at him, then shook her head, "No, I ... I remember sleeping in the tent. I ... I think I was having some kind of ... nightmare! There were ... monsters, chasing us, it ... it seemed so real!"

Timothy leaned forward and cradled Jenny's head in his arms.

"That's all it was," Timothy said, "a nightmare. It's all over now ... it's okay now."

There was a noise behind him and Timothy looked round. The door to the orange ship opened and Klaus came staggering in.

"Klaus!" Timothy cried out, standing up and running over to him. Yuki stared at Klaus with a concerned look and ran over to hold his arm helping him to stand.

"Are you okay?" Timothy asked, taking Klaus' other arm.

Klaus nodded, and together both Yuki and Timothy helped him over to the wide sofa-like seat and sat him down nearby Jenny.

"What happened?" Timothy asked, as Jenny sat staring at Klaus curiously.

"My ... my father," Klaus managed to say. "He seemed to be ... sucking the life out of my body!"

Jenny stood up and glanced at Timothy, "Who is this?" she asked.

She gazed around at the strange-looking interior of the ship. "And ... and where the hell are we?" she added, raising her voice in frustration at being given no answers.

"Long story," Timothy said, looking at her.

"You should tell her the truth," Yuki said.

Julia glanced at Yuki, then back to Timothy, "She's right Tim! Please! Tell me the truth!"

# PART 52

Gloria, who was leading the freed prisoners along the road, suddenly stopped.

"What is it?" asked a young man standing beside her.

The moon shone brightly in the dark night sky above as Gloria remained still, squinting her eyes and trying to perceive what was on the road in front of them.

"Stay here," she said, turning to the others behind her.

The small group of freed prisoners watched as Gloria walked slowly forward along the road holding her laser gun ready to fire. As she neared the shapes lying in the road, she became aware of what they were. Bodies. Dead bodies of people from the village. They lay strewn across the road in front of her. She paused, both shock and sadness showing in her expression. She continued to move forward staring down at the bodies as she stepped over and around them. Suddenly, she stopped, staring down at one of the dead bodies lying on the road to her right. Rose lay still with her eyes open, gazing up unseeing at the dark sky above. Gloria remained for a moment, staring down at her, then moved on, stepping over a few more bodies, and then she saw Sharn. She paused, gazing down at him. There was a moment of silence, then Gloria heard a noise behind her and turned. She saw the freed prisoners now moving among the bodies, looking down at them and sobbing. Gloria stood watching them. She noticed Thomas, the elderly man, kneel down beside Rose and begin to sob as he touched her face gently ."Rose ... Rose," he said, his tears falling onto her dead body.

Gloria felt an enormous sadness rise up inside her, it enveloped her, overwhelmed her. She closed her eyes tightly, and tears began to run from them, falling onto her cheeks.

Candor ran as fast as he could on his short stubby legs.

"Go! Go!" he shouted at the freed prisoners running through the forest in front of him. "Don't stop for anything!"

The growls of the zombies, who were chasing them through the forest behind, were growing louder.

Candor glanced back and stopped running He saw at least eight zombies coming through the trees towards him, and turned back to the freed prisoners who were continuing to run up ahead in front of him.

"Get to the road!" he shouted to them. "Get out through the barrier! Go!"

He watched them running away, then turned to face the approaching zombies. They moved closer, growling at him angrily.

Candor picked up a stick from the ground nearby and then stood staring up at them.

"I always found you disgusting!" he said.

Then he let out a loud cry and ran towards them raising the stick in his hand.

Julia sat on the grass nearby a stream gazing across at the road that led into the forest. Both she, and the villagers who had survived the vampire attack, were now safely outside the barrier. The remaining villagers were resting on the grass nearby her, their heads lowered sadly as they stared blankly downwards thinking of their families and friends they had left behind. Suddenly, Julia saw in the darkness something, or someone, farther along the road coming towards them. She stood up, squinting her eyes trying to see who or what it was. After a moment, she was able to make out people walking along the road. The villagers nearby her also stood up to see what Julia was staring at. The dark shapes moved slowly along the road towards them. Julia stepped forward, staring fixedly at them, then she recognized Gloria as the first of the dark shapes.

"Gloria!" she cried out, running forward to greet her, "Gloria!"

Gloria, who had been walking with her head lowered, now looked up. She saw Julia running towards her. A smile broke through the sadness on her face.

"Julia!" she called, and then Julia reached her and threw her arms around her hugging her tightly. The villagers were now running forward to greet the freed prisoners, shouting and crying out with joy, as they were reunited with their families and friends. They cried in each other's arms hugging and kissing each other.

"Let's cross over to the stream!" Julia said to Gloria, pointing the grassy area in front of the stream. "That's where the barrier ends! You can't see it, I wouldn't have known, but the villagers know where it is."

Julia gazed into Gloria's eyes for a moment, "Sharn ... " she began to say.

Gloria nodded, "I saw him," she said sadly.

"And Klaus?" Julia asked.

Gloria glanced down, "He stayed behind to rescue another group of prisoners. I ... I was wrong about him."

Julia stared at her, then she leaned forward and hugged her tightly.

"Let's get the people through the barrier and over near the stream," she said.

# PART 53

"The bomb ... " Klaus said weakly, gazing up at Timothy. "You ... must ...

detonate ... "

"The bomb?" Timothy repeated.  But ... what about the others? Shouldn't we wait? ... Klaus? ... Klaus?"

Klaus seemed to be fighting to keep his eyes open, then his eyes closed and he fell back on the sofa-like seat and now lay completely unconscious.  Timothy stared down at him, then turned to Yuki.

"He ... he wants me to detonate the bomb!" he said.

Yuki nodded, "Sharn showed us what to do," she said.

"You're going to detonate a bomb?" Julia asked, staring at him as if he were crazy.

Timothy looked at her, then nodded, "It's the only way," he said.  "We have to stop this madness.  What happened to you could happen to others if we don't end this now. You're nightmare was real Jenny ... it was real!"

Jenny stared back at him in silence.

Timothy turned to Yuki, "Stay here, look after Jenny and Klaus, I'll be back!"

Yuki nodded and watched as Timothy grabbed Jenny tightly in his arms, kissed her, and then picked up the bomb from the circular control console and turned to leave.

"Timmy!" Jenny called.

Yuki touched a switch on the controls and the ships door slid open. Timothy glanced back at Jenny one last time, then he went out through the door. Yuki pressed the same switch and the door close. Jenny remained still staring at the ship's closed door, then she glanced across at Yuki and shook her head.

"I ... I can't believe this!" she said. "It ... it's too ... "

"Incredible to believe?" Yuki said, finishing Jenny's sentence for her.

Jenny nodded, "Y ... yes!"

"You'd better believe it," Yuki said, "because it's real.'

Yuki regarded Jenny for a moment in silence, then glanced across to Klaus who lay unconscious on the other side of the ship's control room.

"You want proof?" Yuki said, turning back to Jenny.

She walked across to where Klaus lay.

"Come here," she said to Jenny.

Jenny stared at her for a moment, then went over to join her. When Jenny reached her, Yuki turned to Klaus, reached down and pulled apart his lips.

"You see that?" Yuki asked.

Jenny gasped as she stared down at the two fangs now visible in Klaus' mouth.

Jenny stepped back in horror, "My ... my God!" she uttered. "He ... he's a ... "

"A vampire," Yuki said, finishing Jenny's sentence for her. "But don't worry, Klaus is on our side. He's helping us. The bomb Timothy has is a mini-nuclear device. It's going to kill them all. The vampires and the zombies, the monsters you thought were just a nightmare. The blast will be contained within the force field shield surrounding this area which is their prison, so no one outside will get hurt."

"My God ... " Jenny said, glancing down and placing her hand over her mouth, "it ... it's real!"

She remained still for a moment, then looked back up at Yuki, "But ... but what about Timothy? What about us? If the bomb explodes ... " Jenny stared blankly, unable to finish her sentence.

"Don't worry," Yuki said.

She walked back over to the control console and flipped a switch. The screen on the wall came into focus showing the large moonlit clearing outside the ship. Jenny looked up at the screen and saw Timothy running across to the centre of the clearing with the bomb in his hands.

"This is a Spaceship," Yuki continued, "stroke, Time Machine. When Timothy comes back, we should be able to leave."

Candor lay dead on the ground as the zombies ran forward over his small dead body chasing the freed prisoners running through the forest in front of them. Twigs snapped and branches broke as they ran jerkily through the trees growling loudly and angrily, and then suddenly, they stopped. They stared through the remaining trees at the road just a few yards in front of where they now stood. They growled watching the freed prisoners running through the darkness along the road, then they turned and went back through the trees.

Both Gloria and Julia glanced up as they heard the villagers nearby shouting and pointing towards the road leading into the forest. They stood up and saw more freed prisoners come running along the road towards them. Some of the villagers ran forward onto the road to help and greet them. As the small group came over to the stream and either knelt down or collapsed onto the grass, both Gloria and Julia went over to them. Gloria approached a young girl in ragged clothes and with scratch marks on her body and knelt down beside her.

"Was it a young vampire who helped you escape?" Gloria asked.

The girl stared at her blankly for a moment, then nodded.

"Klaus!" Gloria said, glancing up at Julia.  She turned back to the young girl, "Where is he?" she asked.

"He ... was injured," the young girl said.  "He ... said he had to ... go somewhere ... do something.  We ... we barely managed to escape ... the zombies ... "

Julia glanced at Gloria with a worried look, "He's gone back to detonate the bomb," she said.

Gloria stood up, "If he's injured, he might not make it back."

"Then Timothy or Yuki will detonate it," Julia said.

Gloria looked at her, "I have to make sure," she said, after  moment.  "I have to go back!"

"You're going back?" Julia asked in amazement.  "We barely made it out alive!"

"Julia," Gloria said, gazing into Julia's eyes, "if the bomb isn't detonated, this will never be finished.  I have to make sure!  I have to go back!"

Julia grabbed her arm as Gloria was about to turn away.

"Gloria ... " she said.

"You're free now," Gloria said, looking into Julia's eyes.  "You can go home, you can forget about this."

Julia shook her head, "I ... I will never forget about this!" she said.

Gloria smiled at her, "Take care Julia," she said, then she turned and walked back across to the road leading into the forest.

"You're crazy!" Julia shouted out to her. "Do you know that?"

Julia remained still, watching her go.

Gloria walked fast along the road, grasping the laser gun tightly in her hands, a grim determined look on her face. Suddenly, she heard a noise behind her and turned. Julia came running up to her.

"If you think I'm going to let you go back there alone, you're mistaken!" Julia said, now walking along the road beside her.

Gloria looked at her and smiled.

Timothy stopped running and glanced around as he now walked to the centre of the large clearing. He stopped, looking at the surrounding trees in the darkness, listening to the rustling of the leaves in the breeze, then he placed the bomb down onto the ground in front of him. He stood for a moment, staring down at it, then he bent down. He glanced back at the bright orange triangular ship on the other side of the clearing thinking of Jenny who was now back to normal and safely inside it. Apart from the breeze rustling the leaves, there was an eerie silence in the darkness of the night as he remained still. He thought of Gloria, Julia and Sharn and hoped that they had time to get out through the barrier with the villagers and the prisoners. Finally, he glanced back down at the bomb on the grass just in front of him. Slowly, he reached towards it, his hand shaking as he stared down at the bomb's switch nervously. And then he heard a noise to his right.

# PART 54

Both Gloria and Julia ran through the dark forest, stopping occasionally and hiding behind trees as they heard and saw zombies nearby. Each time they waited, then continued on through the forest as fast as they could.

"We're approaching the clearing!" Gloria called back to Julia, who was following behind, but before Julia could answer, she stumbled over something and fell. Gloria heard her cry and ran back to help her up. As she reached her, she could see that Julia was staring wide-eyed at something on the ground. Gloria looked to where Julia was staring and saw the mutilated half-eaten body of the hunchback. Gloria stifled a gasp. Both of them stared down at the body for a moment, then Gloria turned to Julia to help her up. As Julia stood up she continued to stare down at the ghastly sight of the hunchback's mutilated body.

"Come on!" Gloria said, pulling on Julia's arm. "We've got to go!"

Together, they turned away from the body and once again started to run through the trees now hearing growling sounds in the darkness both to their right and to their left as they ran.

Timothy saw the zombies standing on the edge of the clearing staring towards him. There was one zombie he recognized among them. It was Klaus' uncle, or rather, what was left of his uncle. The creature's green eyes shone brightly in the darkness as it growled, observing him. Timothy raised the laser gun he had carried from the ship and aimed carefully at Green Eyes who remained still, growling and snarling towards him like some wild animal. Suddenly, Green Eyes began to move forward across the clearing towards him while the other zombies remained still, watching. Timothy began to sweat, his hands gripping the laser gun tightly began to shake. He waited nervously until Green Eyes, who was moving slowly across the clearing, now grinning and seeming to savor each passing moment as he came, was closer, and then he fired.

Nothing happened.

"Oh hell!" Timothy said to himself, pressing the trigger on the laser gun again and again.

Green Eyes grin grew wider as he came closer. Helplessly, Timothy lowered the laser gun and watched with wide fear-filled eyes as Green Eyes now began to move faster towards him.

Jenny and Yuki both watched what was happening on the ship's screen.

"Oh my God!" Jenny shouted, raising her hands to her mouth. "I … I've got to help him!"

She looked quickly around for something, anything, that she could use to help him. She saw a sword that had been previously discarded and ran across to pick it up.

"Jenny!" Yuki called to her. "What ... what are you doing?"

Jenny picked up the sword and ran towards the door.

"I've got to help him! Open the door!"

"Jenny ... !" Yuki cried. "You'll get yourself killed!"

Jenny turned to her, "Open this God damn door!" she shouted back at Yuki.

Yuki stared at her, then nodded quickly and pressed a switch on the console to open the door. The door slid open and Jenny ran out as fast as she could into the night.

# PART 55

Timothy cried out, now swinging his laser gun at the approaching zombie. He hit Green Eyes on the head but it seemed to have no effect on him. Green Eyes stopped moving and stared at him. A moment of silence passed between them as they stared at each other, then Timothy raised the laser gun again using it as a club. He swung the laser gun towards Green Eyes but Green Eyes swatted it effortlessly away with his arm and then growled reaching forward with its clawed fingers towards Timothy. Timothy staggered back and tripped, falling to the ground. He lay, frozen, staring up at the approaching green-eyed monster with horror-filled eyes. Green Eyes fell onto him, clasping its green fingers around Timothy's neck. Timothy cried out, he screamed loudly, and then Green Eyes leaned forward towards his neck and bit it.

"Aaaaaaaargh!" Jenny screamed, running up behind the hideous creature and raising the sword in her hands. But before she could strike, Green Eyes turned and lashed out with an arm, hitting her and knocking her back off her feet. Jenny fell, the sword falling to the ground beside her. Green Eyes stood up and moved over to her. Jenny stared up at the monster who now stood above her, staring down at her with its bright green eyes. It growled and Jenny screamed as Green Eyes reached own and picked her up effortlessly. Green Eyes leaned back its head, seemed to growl loudly up at the moon as Jenny screamed, trapped in the monster's grip, and then it leaned forward, opened its mouth widely, and bit into Jenny's throat. Blood spurted out covering the monster's face as Jenny stopped screaming. She now hung lifeless in the monsters grip, staring up wide-eyed at the dark night sky with unseeing eyes as her body began to move spasmodically. Green Eyes stared at her, then let go. Jenny's body fell to the ground like a lifeless doll, the blood gushing out of her throat and onto the grass all around her. Green Eyes once again leaned its head back and growled loudly up at the moon. Suddenly, it saw something from the corner of its eye and turned. But it was too late. Timothy screamed raising the sword in both hands and swung it at Green-Eyes neck. The sharp blade bit into its neck severing it completely and its head fell away from its body and onto the ground. Timothy watched as Green-Eyes' head rolled along the grass and its body fell lifelessly down. The head stopped rolling face upwards, and Timothy saw the bright light from its green eyes dim, and then finally go out. Timothy dropped the sword, then turned to stare down at Jenny. He took two steps forward, then fell down beside her body. Gently, he raised her head and gazed down at her face with tears in his eyes, and then, he began to sob.

"Jenny! ... Jenny!" he cried, his body shaking as he clutched her body tightly in his arms.

He heard wild animal-like growls and looked up. There, on the other side of the clearing, he saw about thirty zombies growling wildly towards him. Suddenly he heard someone call his name far off to his right and turned.

"Timothy! Timothy!" Gloria was calling towards him, running out from the trees at the other end of the clearing.

He saw Julia run out of the trees behind her. They were both running towards the bright orange ship. Suddenly, Timothy felt something happening to his face. Something was changing inside him. He looked down at his hands. They were turning white, his skin was beginning to crack. Green Eyes' bite to his neck! Timothy thought. Timothy realized that he was being transformed into a zombie, just like Jenny had been. He glanced down at the bomb lying on the ground just a few feet away, then looked back towards Gloria and Julia who had now stopped running towards the orange ship and were now standing still, staring at him.

"Go!" Timothy shouted out, waving his arm and gesturing for them to continue running towards the ship, "Go! Go!"

Timothy turned and saw the long line of zombies now steadily approaching him. Gloria was about to run forward towards him but Julia caught her arm.

"Gloria!" Julia said urgently. "We can't do anything! We have to go!"

Gloria remained staring towards Timothy and watched as he turned back to the bomb lying just a few feet away from him.

"Gloria! Let's go!" Julia shouted, pulling on Gloria's arm.

Reluctantly, Gloria turned and ran with Julia over towards the orange ship. Timothy leaned down and picked up the mini nuclear bomb. He glanced across to the other side of the clearing at both Gloria and Julia and saw that they had now reached the orange ship. Julia had entered, but Gloria paused, looking back at him before disappearing inside. Timothy turned to look at the approaching zombies. A smile now came onto his face which was rapidly turning white.

"This is for Jenny," he said, and then pressed the buttons on the side of the bomb, putting in the code for destruction. He paused on the last button glancing up towards the orange ship on the far side of the clearing. He heard the now familiar machine-like noise coming from it, and then watched as it began to disappear. Timothy looked back at the approaching zombies, gave them one last smile, then pressed the final button. The bomb exploded with the force of a nuclear bomb devastating, everything within the confines of the invisible barrier.

# PART 56

"Where are we going?" Julia asked, looking across the circular console at Yuki who was manipulating the controls as if she knew exactly what she was doing.

"She ... the ship ... speaks to me," Yuki said. "I know how to use this. We're going back, we're going back to save them."

Gloria, who was leaning against the console with her head lowered sadly and thinking of Timothy, looked up at her.

"Going back?" she said.

"Do you mean ... " Julia said, staring across at Yuki, "... going back, in time?"

Yuki nodded, pushing various buttons on the controls in front of her.

"It's done!" she said finally.

"How's that possible?" Gloria asked. "I ... I thought this was a Spaceship ... I ... I thought we couldn't go back."

Yuki shrugged, "The ship says we can. Er ... by the way, I've given her a name."

"Pardon?" Julia said, staring at her in surprise.

"Crystal!" Yuki said, with a smile on her face. "The ship gets its power from certain crystals, so I've called her Crystal. She seems to like it!"

Julia gazed at her sideways, "I always knew you were weird!" she said.

Gloria looked across at Klaus, who was still lying unconscious on the wide sofa-like seat.

"How's Klaus?" she asked, stepping over towards him.

"He was injured," Yuki said. "He said his father was ... sucking the life out of him."

"Will he be okay?" Julia asked.

Yuki nodded, "I think so," she said. "I think he just needs rest."

Suddenly, the machine-like whirring sound of the ship grew louder.

"What's happening?" Julia said, grasping onto the console for support as the ship began to vibrate.

"We're landing," Yuki said.

The loud whirring machine-like sound and the vibrations shaking the ship strongly continued, and then, after a few moments, everything abruptly stopped.

Each of them remained still, breathing heavily in the following silence, and then they looked up at the screen.

We've landed," Gloria said.

It was a bright sunny Summer's day. Timothy was busy trying to put up a tent in the clearing of the woods, and he seemed to be losing the battle. Jenny laughed, strolling across the clearing towards him.

"Have a nice walk?" Timothy said, as she approached him.

"Haven't you put up that tent yet?" Jenny said. "I thought it'd be ready by now. I was looking forward to climbing inside and having a nap."

"Well, thank you for your help!" Timothy said, glancing at her. You know, if I didn't know any better, I'd say that this thing was alive and it doesn't like me!"

Suddenly, part of the tent that Timothy had put up collapsed. Jenny laughed again.

"Funny huh?" Timothy said, looking at her as she continued to laugh. "You know, I told you before we came on this trip that I'm not the outdoor type."

Jenny moved forward to take over putting up the tent.

"Oh come on!" she said. "Move over! Let me do it!"

Timothy put his hands on his hips watching her.

"Oh? So you think you can do better, do you?" Timothy asked.

"Yep!" Jenny said, beginning to erect the tent as if she knew exactly what she was doing.

"Oh!" Timothy said, watching her. "That bit ... goes there?"

Jenny looked at him and laughed again as she continued to put the tent up without any problems.

"Excuse me!" Came a voice from behind them.

Both Timothy and Jenny turned to see two girls walking across the clearing towards them. The girl with the blonde shoulder-length hair seemed a little older than the other girl who had short black hair and who looked to be in her late teens. Both girls seemed strange especially the younger girl who appeared to be a Goth. They stared at the younger girl's torn clothes wondering if it was some kind of new Goth-like fashion. The girls stopped in front of them and the blonde-haired girl smiled as she spoke.

"I wouldn't camp in these woods if I were you," the blonde-haired girl said.

"Oh? Really?" Timothy said, studying them both strangely. "Why not?"

Both the blonde girl and the teen-aged Goth looked at each other.

"Er ... rabies!" the Goth girl said. "Yes, er ... most of the animals here are, er ... infected with it."

Rabies?" Jenny repeated. "But ... we haven't heard anything about rabies."

"Oh, yes!" the blonde-haired girl said. "It's ... quite rife in the area. I'm surprised you haven't heard about it. Just the other day, one of our friends was bitten by a ... a ..."

"A mole!" Julia said, finishing Gloria's sentence for her.

Gloria glanced at her, a little surprised at Julia's inventiveness, then she looked back at both Timothy and Jenny, "Er ... yes!" she said. "That's right. A mole!"

She stared down sadly, "Bad business! Don't know if she'll survive the night actually."

"Oh, we ... we're sorry to hear that," Jenny said.

Timothy glanced at her, "See? The outdoor life? I knew we should have stayed at a hotel!"

Jenny sighed, then shrugged, "Well, there's that Inn we saw as we passed through the village. Maybe we could go there."

"The Slaughtered Lamb?" Gloria said, staring at them both.

"Er ... maybe that's not a good idea either," Julia said. "If I were you, I'd just leave this area altogether, you know, go somewhere else, completely different."

"My friend's right," Gloria said. "I wouldn't want to run the risk of staying here if I were you."

Both Timothy and Jenny glanced at each other. Timothy shrugged, "Okay!" he said, looking back at them, "That's fine by me! Thanks for the advice!"

"You're welcome," Gloria said with a smile.

Then both Gloria and Julia turned and walked away. Timothy and Jenny watched them walk back across the clearing, then Timothy turned to Jenny, "I'm going to pack up this tent!" he said, with a big grin on his face.

When they had reached the other side of the clearing both Gloria and Julia looked back and saw Timothy and Jenny packing up and preparing to leave.

"A mole?" Gloria said, looking at Julia with a smile on her face. "Seriously?"

Julia shrugged, "What? It was all I could think of!" she said defensively.

# PART 57

Back in the orange ship, Julia sat down to check on Klaus.

"He's breathing better," she said.

Yuki looked at Gloria, "Well? Did it work?" she asked.

Gloria nodded and sat down with a sigh, "Yes, it worked," she said. "We changed the past."

Julia glanced at her, "Not for the Timothy and Jenny we knew," she said. "What we did was create another version of what happened, and therefore ... another dimension. Sharn explained that."

Gloria nodded, "Yes, I know. The Timothy and Jenny we knew are still dead. But ... those two we met, their lives will branch off into a different dimension, and they will live."

Julia leaned back and sighed, "Well, anyway, I hope they'll be happy."

Yuki stood studying them both from nearby the console, "So ... where to now?" she asked. "I could set the controls to go back and save your sister," she said, now looking at Gloria.

Gloria stared at her for a moment, "You ... you can do that?" she asked.

"Of course!" Yuki said. "Just give me the date and time! I know the place."

Gloria stood up and went over to her.

"Yuki, if you could do that, that would

be ... " suddenly she stopped speaking.

"What is it?" Julia asked, now standing up and walking back over to join her.

"It ... it could change everything," Gloria said, gazing down thoughtfully. She looked back up at Julia, "Everything that

happened!" she added.

"You don't know that," Julia said. "If Sharn was right, you'll be creating another dimension, and you'll get your sister back."

"And if he wasn't right?" Gloria said. "We could undo everything we've done."

Julia reached out and squeezed Gloria's arm gently, "We could still try," she said.

"But ... what would happen?" Gloria asked, looking at her. "What would be the consequences? If Sharn wasn't right?"

There was a moment of silence as they gazed at each other thoughtfully. Yuki, who was studying them both, turned towards the console.

"I'm going to try!" she said. "Gloria, give me the time and date!"

Gloria looked at her for a moment, hesitating.

"What about you Yuki?" Gloria said. "Don't you want to go back to something?"

Yuki gazed around at the interior of the ship, and then smiled, "Me? I feel good right here. Now, give me the date and time!"

Gloria paused.

"Try," Julia said, urging her on with a smile.

Gloria looked at her, then nodded, "Okay. The ... the 8th of April," she said. "About ... 10 o'clock in the morning."

"Right!" Yuki said.

She touched the controls, set the date and time, and then pressed various buttons before pulling a lever. The ship started its loud machine-like sound and then began to vibrate. As moments passed, the sound grew louder, and the vibrations grew stronger. The whole ship began to shake violently, smoke began to rise up from the console as the sound now seemed almost unbearable. Each of them pressed their hands to their ears, falling to the floor as they did so.

"What's happening?" Julia shouted across to Yuki.

"I don't know!" Yuki shouted back. "There's something wrong!"

Suddenly, the vibrations and the almost ear-splitting sound ceased, and each of them lay on the floor in silence breathing heavily.

"What the hell just happened?" Julia asked, looking across at Yuki. "You said it speaks to you! What does it say?"

Yuki pulled herself up onto her feet. She cocked her head to one side as if she were listening. Both Gloria and Julia watched her as they too got up onto their feet.

"Well?" Julia asked.

Yuki looked at her, then shook her head, "Nothing," she said. "She's not saying anything!"

Gloria stepped forward looking up at the screen. At first, the image seemed out of focus, and then it began to clear.

"Well ... we've arrived somewhere," she said.

"But where?" Julia asked, staring up at the image on the screen.

The orange ship had materialized in a field. The sun was shining and the sky was blue, it seemed to be a beautiful day. The ship's door slid open and both Gloria and Julia stepped out.

"Wow! It looks like we did it!" Julia said, gazing around at the surrounding forest.

Gloria walked forward and saw that they were in a field on a hill over-looking a beautiful landscape.

"Er ... I'm not so sure," Gloria said, gazing down at something strange she'd seen in the landscape far below them.

"What do you mean?" Julia asked, coming over to stand beside her.

Gloria pointed down to the landscape beneath the hill. Julia took two steps forward staring down to where Gloria was pointing. Suddenly, she froze.

"Er ... is that what I think it is?" Julia asked.

She turned to look back at Gloria.

Gloria nodded, "It's a dinosaur," she said.

In the landscape far below them, they saw a dinosaur drinking from a flowing river.

Julia looked back down at the dinosaur, her mouth opening wide in both surprise and shock, and then saw another, and then another.

She glanced back at Gloria, "This is crazy!" she said. "Just ... just how far back have we come?"

Gloria studied the prehistoric landscape below with a grin, "I'd say pretty far," she said.

Suddenly, Yuki came running out of the ship behind them.

They both turned to her.

"What is it?" Gloria asked.

"It's Crystal!" she said. "The ship! I ... I think its ill! It's rambling! It's rambling on saying something about its sister, its sister ship!"

Gloria stared at her, "Its ... sister ship?" she repeated in amazement.

Far far away, on another planet, in another time, another large, bright orange, and triangular ship materialized on top of a hill.

The door slid open and Sinella stepped out followed by a small group of vampires.

"We've been waiting for you!" said a tall thin vampire who had apparently been waiting on the hilltop for their arrival. "Where's the other ship?" the vampire asked. "Where's Erik?"

Sinella regarded him, then shook her head sadly, "Erik's dead," she said. "This is the only ship. The other ship had problems. Is everything ready?"

The vampire who had been waiting for them nodded, "Everything's ready," he said. "Come, see for yourself."

They followed him across the hill until they reached a place where they had a view of the landscape below them. Far below, at least two thousand vampires stood in ranks as if they were in the military.

"Behold!" the tall thin vampire said.

 "A vampire army!"

He raised his arm and all of the two-thousand strong vampires below raised their fists in a salute and cheered.

Sinella smiled, gazing down at the vampire army below them.

"You have done well Keno," she said.  "You have done very well indeed!"

The
End

# ABOUT THE AUTHOR

Lawrence Nabbs (Larry) was born in London, England. He wrote his first short story at the age of eleven. He later started to write poems and other short stories. He was given the idea for his first novel length story after having had the strange experience of seeing UFOs in France. Since then, Larry has enjoyed writing novel length stories, but still writes poems from time to time. In England, he did different jobs, not really finding himself until he went to Paris, France, to become an English teacher where he lived and worked as a teacher for over twenty years, therefore he also speaks French. He later went to Beijing, China, in the year 2006 where he continues to teach English and write novel length stories, such as crime thrillers, science fiction and fantasies. He has also written stories for a children's comic in China for learning English. He loves the cinema, films of all kinds, as well as books and music. He likes and very often writes stories in cafes, and also loves the feeling of being near the ocean.